Masterpiece of Deception

Masterpiece

of

Deception

AN ART MYSTERY

by

Judy Lester

SUMACH
PRESS

To Patti Sniderman,
the very first of my life-long friends.

NATIONAL LIBRARY OF CANADA CATALOGUING IN PUBLICATION DATA

Lester, Judy

Masterpiece of deception: an art mystery

ISBN 1-894549-10-4

I. Title

PS8573.E789M38 2001   C813'.6   C2001-902019-8
PR199.4.L48M38 2001

COVER IMAGE: Cross section of a paint sample (in ultra violet illumination) from the overpainted sky of *Diana en haar nymphen (Diana and Her Companions)* by Johannes Vermeer, c. 1655. M.H. Inv. no. 406. Courtesy of the Conservation Studio, Royal Cabinet of paintings Mauritshuis, The Hague.

Printed in Canada

Published by

SUMACH PRESS
1415 Bathurst Street, Suite 202
Toronto ON M5R 3H8
sumachpress@on.aibn.com

www.sumachpress.com

Acknowledgements

I am grateful to many individuals who have provided me with help and encouragement. For direct assistance I wish to thank Susan Carlyle, Grace Gray, Robert Barclay, Guillaume Sylvestre, Donna Mehos, Jaap Boon, Régine Page, Vicki Davis, Paddy O'Connor, and Patrick Nee. For encouragement with early drafts, I am grateful to Jane Down, Patti Sniderman, Ela and Bob Keyserlingk, Anne Ruggles, Ilona Hurda, Sandra Lafortune, David Grattan, Lynda Woodroffe, and Debora Dyer. I am especially indebted to David Tremain who suggested and provided essential background reading and information. I also wish to thank my colleagues in the Conservation Processes and Materials Research Division at the Canadian Conservation Institute who have been enthusiastic contributors over coffee breaks. Thanks to Sue Bronston, George Lovitt, and Sally Warren for their help with my first steps in finding a publisher and to Jane Down who put me in touch with Sumach Press. For assistance with technical details, I am grateful to Detective-Sergeant Alain Lacoursiére, art-fraud specialist with the Montreal Urban Community Police; to Brent Binnie, Chief-Prevention/Canadian Forces Base, Suffield; and to Christopher Roche, Division Chief, Training, Ottawa Fire Department. Any inaccuracies are the author's responsibility. I am very grateful to Sumach Press and Marcia Sweet for their help and support with this first novel, and to my colleague Petria Noble, Senior Conservator, Conservation Department, Mauritshuis, The Hague, for kindly supplying the cross-section for the cover image.

My knowledge of many of the fine locations Jerry visited, is thanks to the generous friendship of Grace and George Gray, and Mari and Peter Bicknell. For Dolceacqua I am grateful to Lucie Vary. My heartfelt thanks to Claude Sylvestre, who, in the spirit of Willy, Colette's husband, kept me fed and shut up in my room till it was finished.

AUTHOR'S NOTE

The Chelsea Institute of Art, the Charles Haverstock Institute, and the South Kensington Museum are fictitious, as are all the characters in the book. I have invented freely for the sake of the story, and have simplified some of the technical details. For example, the question of whether or not to use a natural or synthetic varnish is far more complex, and there are more options available than I have described. Vermeer's painting of *Diana and Her Companions* does exist and is in the collection of the Mauritshuis in The Hague. I am most grateful to Petria Noble at the Mauritshuis who kindly made a cross-section from this painting available for the cover design.

Tony and Alvin do exist and have been described faithfully (although Alvin's name was changed to ensure his anonymity). The reader is assured that while some humans in this story may meet a nasty end, neither cat is hurt in any way.

Chapter 1

JERRY SAT BACK IN HER CHAIR WITH A SIGH. The seventeenth-century painting on the easel in front of her just did not make sense. The more she studied it, the less sure she felt about what she was seeing. That it had been extensively repainted was obvious, but what was becoming less obvious was what belonged to the original old painting and what had been added. At first she had thought the restoration would be straightforward. Someone had painted over the Dutch landscape using acrylic paint, easy to date and easy to remove. But as she removed the acrylic, she was becoming increasingly uneasy.

"It just doesn't add up," she said irritably. She stood up, stretched, and walked over to the kitchen to boil water for tea. Alvin, who had been curled up on a stool by the counter, became instantly alert at the possibility of a fresh snack. Jerry stroked him absentmindedly. With a quiet and hopeful "mrrumph" he tentatively turned on the charm, but her mind was obviously elsewhere.

Jerry was worried. If this painting turned out to be more complicated than she had anticipated, her initial estimate for the cost of restoring it would be seriously off. Her loan repayments for the studio equipment she had had to purchase were steep. As much as she wanted to hurry the work along, as a professional restorer she knew she could not cut corners.

"Well," she said going to the fridge for some milk, "I definitely need more time with this one to sort it out. Don't you agree, Alvin?" But Alvin wasn't listening; he had just caught sight of Tony who had appeared at the sound of the fridge door opening.

What I need is a *real* job, she thought, a nice regular paycheque, from a nice regular highly prestigious public institution. If I win the competition for that position at the museum, it will solve everything. With my background I must have looked good to the interview panel. What's taking them so long to decide? She warmed the teapot with some hot water and surveyed the loft where her studio and apartment were combined. Even though the old building was in an isolated industrial area and she was the only person living there, the rest taken up with a warehouse, she did not regret her decision to move here a year ago. The light was perfect. Huge windows in the studio and kitchen opened onto a balcony, which ran along the front of the building. Enormously high ceilings gave the impression of a large space, which was enhanced by the way the studio had been left open to the kitchen in the recent renovation, creating a single bright room spanning the entire width of the loft. The only downside was the living room and bedroom, which ran across the back of the building. Despite the ceiling height, they could still only be described as "cozy." Her thoughts were interrupted as Alvin let out a howl of outrage; Tony was getting altogether too close to his food dish.

Just then, her friend Carol, who often dropped in on her way home from work, pushed open the large front door. She found Jerry on the kitchen floor trying to pacify the two growling and hissing cats.

"Honestly, Jerry, why don't you give up? Those two are never going to make peace with each other. It's hopeless."

Jerry looked up and smiled. "I'm glad to see you," she said as she stood up and brushed herself off. "I've just run into something peculiar about this painting. I'd really like your opinion."

Carol had been trained as a restorer, but not long after graduation she had taken a job in the registration department at the Toronto museum where Jerry had recently applied for a position. She had confessed to Jerry that she did not have the nerve required to clean the delicate surfaces of valuable paintings. Despite her reluctance to actually treat a painting, she had a keen eye and her insight into artists' methods had been very useful to Jerry more than once. Jerry appreciated being able to bounce her ideas off Carol, especially with this piece, the most puzzling she had ever encountered.

Jerry's stereomicroscope stood in front of the painting. Designed for eye surgeons, the powerful stereovision provided by the microscope allowed her to inspect the paint surface at high magnification, while its long working distance meant she had enough room to manoeuvre underneath it, easily able to guide her hands as she made microscopic tests with solvents on the surface of the painting. Mounted on a tall vertical stand with a heavy base and locking wheels, the microscope itself could be tilted to almost any angle. At that moment, it was positioned close to the paint surface at its maximum magnification.

Taking turns looking through the stereomicroscope, she and Carol discussed what they were seeing. Acrylic overpaint covered large areas of the dark landscape and was easy to identify. The acrylic colours were overbright, almost glaring, compared with the muted tones of the paint underneath. The texture of the acrylic was relentlessly smooth and the surface slick: there was no mistaking it for genuine old oil paint.

"What shlock-work," said Carol disgustedly, as she stood back from the microscope and looked at the whole painting as it sat on the easel. She picked up a photograph taken before Jerry had started to remove the acrylic paint. "Who would do this awful overpainting?"

"You're right, it's terrible," replied Jerry. "But what I really want your opinion on is this." She pointed to paint that had been revealed where she had removed the top coat of acrylic. "The surface isn't right. Don't you think it's strange?"

Before she readjusted the microscope to have a closer look, Carol pulled back her mass of curly blond hair to get it away from her face and wrapped it around itself at the nape of her neck in one practised movement. Jerry marvelled at how Carol's hair stayed where it was put. If she tried that, her black hair would immediately unravel, springing back to its one and only place: hanging straight and thick to her shoulders. They could not be more opposite. Carol's exuberant hair was a perfect expression of her personality. She was tall, plump and wore colourful, loose clothing. Jerry, fine boned and slender to the point of thin, sometimes looked liked a waif around Carol, her quiet energy easily extinguished in Carol's presence. But at other times, when she was paying attention, Jerry's looks could take on a sophisticated polish. When it came to competence and determination, Jerry and Carol were equals.

As she waited for Carol to examine the painting, Jerry's thoughts drifted to the museum job again. It would give her the financial security she needed. Her long years of training had left her well in the hole, and at twenty-nine she was tired of living like a student. But the training had been worth it. Even as an undergraduate in art history she had wanted to get much closer to paintings than the typical slide-lectures would allow. She had wanted more, to penetrate the painters' minds: what did they want from their paint? What were they after with the texture? How did some artists get that wonderful pasty effect, that three-dimensional brushwork, while others created a looking-glass surface, magically smooth, the brushwork invisible? What did they do to achieve those effects?

Her art history professors gently advised that her interest in the mechanics of painting was pedestrian and that her insistence that the materials and techniques were important was embarrassingly naive. They suggested she consider studio art instead. Perhaps she'd rather be a painter.

So Jerry took some studio courses, but found herself equally frustrated. Instead of learning about technique, she discovered that in painting classes, to pay too much attention to materials was considered "precious." The idea was to create, the vehicle was secondary. And beneath her professors' disregard for the material were at least two generations of teachers who had never been taught technique themselves. The majority had no idea how painters had worked in the past.

Then she discovered restoration. She could get as involved with the physical side of paintings as she wanted. What could be more intimate than the surface of an old painting at forty-times magnification? Of course it was not easy. She had had to take chemistry courses to qualify to train in restoration. After a steady diet of the arts and humanities, she found chemistry mind-bendingly difficult. She had to adjust her way of thinking radically. But it was also exhilarating, and the physical world itself took on an entirely new meaning.

The phone rang for the third time.

"Jerry! Aren't you going to answer that?" Carol called out.

Snapping out of her reverie, she grabbed the phone.

"Ms. McPherson? This is Dorothy Simpson from the South Kensington Museum in London. You've been selected for an interview for the position of assistant restorer. Are you available to come over next week?"

"Well, yes ... I ... I suppose ... I mean of course!" Jerry stammered as her mind raced. London? Next week! This was certainly not the call she had been expecting.

As Dorothy Simpson sped on with the details, Jerry listened and tried to pay attention. But it was all going by in a blur. She had barely taken it in, then Ms. Simpson was saying goodbye. "We'll be in contact later this week to give you the flight information."

Jerry shook her head in amazement. "Carol, that was from London! They want me to interview for the job at the South Kensington Museum. I can't believe it!"

"Well I can," returned Carol dryly. "You certainly have the qualifications. But what about the museum here, I thought you were aiming for that? I didn't even know you had applied for something in London. You are a mystery sometimes, Jerry."

The truth was, Jerry had thought she wouldn't have a chance at a job in London, so she had applied more on a whim than with any serious intent. She was well aware of the fierce competition in England for such positions. She was convinced that as a North American she would never be considered.

"I'm sorry I didn't tell you, I just didn't think I'd even get an interview. I thought if you knew I was trying for it, and then I found out I didn't get it ... Well, it would have been embarrassing."

It was an awkward moment. She and Carol had few secrets. They had been close friends for a long time, ever since their undergraduate years in art history. But Jerry hadn't wanted her to know about this, especially because it was such a long shot. Carol tended to take on a motherly role that Jerry sometimes found oppressive. She would have wanted to discuss it, to speculate on Jerry's chances. Jerry hadn't wanted to make it that real, then she couldn't get too disappointed if it didn't happen.

Wanting to change the subject, Jerry asked Carol what she thought was happening with the painting now that she had taken a closer look.

"Well, it is very strange, I agree," said Carol slowly. "There's a natural resin varnish over the surface, which you found when you took off the acrylic paint, right? But it's weird the way the varnish is separating from the paint surface. I haven't seen that before. Do you think it's because the paint underneath the varnish is so old?"

"I'm not sure. I find it very puzzling. The varnish seems to have lost adhesion in places, creating air pockets between it and the paint. Anyway, it's not the strangest thing about this painting. Look what happens when I try to remove the varnish with a solvent." Jerry deftly rolled a small tuft of cotton wool around a thin wooden stick.

"This looks like old original seventeenth-century paint here, don't you agree?" She pointed to an area that had been revealed when she took off the nasty acrylic paint. Carol nodded. "Well, watch this." She dipped her tiny cotton swab in a jar of solvent then blotted the cotton tip on a small piece of absorbent paper. Then she rolled the still-moist cotton onto the surface of the painting.

"Oh, my god! What's going on?" cried Carol. Jerry's once white swab had come away tinged with brown paint. On the painting, a tiny spot of bright yellow shone through where seconds ago there had been a uniform brown surface. Carol sat back slowly in her chair, her eyes remained fixed on that small yellow spot.

"What solvent did you use? It must be really powerful stuff!"

"That's just it, Carol. It's not strong at all. Look closely. The solvent wasn't even strong enough to fully dissolve the varnish, most of it just ran underneath and dissolved the paint. I don't care how old this paint looks, there is no way a seventeenth-century painting would respond like this," she finished, sounding worried. Both knew that old paint is highly resistant to the majority of solvents that restorers use to remove varnish. The behaviour of this paint was very odd.

"So, what are we looking at? Is there another image under there?" Carol continued. "But I don't understand. That brown paint from the landscape is so cracked, you never see this kind of cracking in recent paint."

"No, you don't. This one has me really confused," said Jerry.

"Here is a landscape showing every indication of being old, with all the cracks we associate with aged paint, but it's dissolving in the weakest of solvents. Old paint wouldn't budge in a solvent this mild."

They sat in silence looking at the painting. That there was another painting underneath was not what worried them. They knew that it was not unusual to find another image underneath, since artists often reworked or changed a picture as they painted. Sometimes they even reused an old canvas, painting over an earlier image. Furthermore, it was not unknown for others to alter finished paintings. Military personnel were given new uniforms to reflect a change in rank; portraits of women had appearing and disappearing cleavage according to the dictates of fashion. Even religious figures could undergo conversion.

What was strange here was the odd solubility of this "old" paint. It looked like someone had gone to a lot of trouble to make the landscape painting appear much older than it was. Jerry had seen such extensive overpainting only once before: she had restored a nineteenth-century painting that had been almost entirely repainted by a hack "restorer." When she removed the crude overpaint, the reason it was applied became evident. The original paint had disfiguring cracks, called alligatoring, over most of the surface. Instead of taking time to apply paint to the crack lines, a slow and tedious procedure that left the original painting intact, someone had made a quick job of it by slathering modern paint on top of everything. The painting had looked dreadful until she had uncovered the original.

However, with that painting there had been no attempt to disguise the fresh painting and to make the surface appear old. No finesse was involved. The landscape painting Jerry and Carol were examining was quite the opposite. What they saw appeared to be very cunning. It made them wonder what exactly was underneath.

Jerry broke the silence. "Well, now that I'm going to London, I'll be able to talk to my old professor at the Chelsea Art Institute, Dr. Johnson. He's seen everything. When I show him the photographs of this painting, he's bound to be able to help."

Chapter 2

Tony, in response to Jerry's imminent departure for the job interview in London, had just tried to wrap himself around her ankles for the thirtieth time that morning. Despite being neutered soon after he showed up as a stray a year ago, he still bore the vestiges of tom-hood: a thick neck and a muscular compact frame. He reminded Jerry of a bouncer, and at that moment he was making progress difficult as she tried to cross the room to answer the door.

"Really, Tony, try to get a grip!" she said, exasperated. Realizing her poor choice of words she added, "I mean buck up or something. I'm only going to be away for a few days!"

She gave her clothes a quick brush to remove traces of his tabby coat before opening the door.

"Ah, Andrew, I'm so glad you could come by on such short notice," she said as she stepped aside to let him in. "I really wanted you to see the painting before I went away."

Andrew, as impeccably tailored as usual, entered the studio looking fully the part of a successful art dealer. He was a tall handsome man, always courteous and pleasant, but Jerry nevertheless found him a bit unnerving. She thought it was his stiff formality that put her off. Still, she welcomed the business he had brought her in the year since they had met, and she had to admit, he was a good listener when she explained her work to him. In turn, his broad knowledge of the art market, which he occasionally shared, provided her with a perspective on the commercial side of things that she was rarely privy to.

"Here it is. As you can see, I've removed all of the acrylic over-painting," she explained as she led him to the painting where it sat on the easel. She did not volunteer any information. For the time being she wanted to see it through his eyes. She waited patiently by his side as he concentrated on what was in front of him.

Jerry watched Andrew studying the painting. He certainly did make an impressive figure. With his perfectly cut blond hair, beige cashmere overcoat and expensive suit, he could have passed as an important CEO. The only indication that he did not belong to the corporate establishment was his lack of a tie. Instead he sported a black knit polo-shirt underneath his suit jacket.

Finally, he was ready with his verdict. He spoke in a cultivated British accent, "It's rather disappointing, isn't it? Sort of a van Ruisdael in monochrome." He continued, frowning, "Why is it so *brown*? I was hoping for more. Before you took off the acrylic, what we could see of the original appeared much more promising." He picked up an 8-by-10-inch photograph taken before treatment had begun, when the acrylic overpaint obscured much of the image.

"See how delicate the work on the foliage is? It looks ... well ... it looks like the hand of a master. But now that the overpaint is gone and the tone of the piece is so dark, that beautiful treatment of the tree leaves is practically lost, and" — he stepped closer to the easel, scrutinizing individual areas — "the quality of the work is quite uneven, isn't it?"

Andrew turned to look at her. As usual, Jerry found his gaze disconcerting. He seemed to look through her, as if he were focused on something else; a bit like Tony did, in fact.

"All this brown, can't you do anything about it? What about the varnish — it still needs to come off — will that brighten it up?" he asked hopefully. Jerry was surprised. She thought Andrew would be capable of assessing the effect of a discoloured varnish, that he would be able to see as well as she could that the pervasive muddiness of this painting was not the result of a darkened varnish alone.

"The owner is going to be very disappointed," Andrew continued. "He and I both thought we had a contemporary of a Dutch master, a respectable 'school-of,' and now ... well, it looks like a nineteenth-century copy, doesn't it?"

She knew it was time to tell Andrew what she had discovered

about the painting. She described how her attempts to remove the varnish resulted in the paint below dissolving away, and explained that while some nineteenth-century paintings could show sensitivity to the solvents used for varnish removal, this painting was exceptional. Some nineteenth-century painters deliberately added varnish to their paint because they wanted the translucent effect that varnish imparted. They felt that the addition of varnish would produce a paint closer in appearance to that used by the old masters. And, believing that homogeneity in materials was important to avoid cracking, some would choose the same resin for their paint that they used for the final varnish.

Andrew broke in to ask, "But if they used the same resin in the paint and in the varnish, wouldn't the solvent used to dissolve the varnish also dissolve the paint?"

She nodded. "In theory, but in practice the paint is usually only partially soluble." She continued, "By carefully adjusting solvent mixtures, a properly trained restorer can ease off the varnish without damaging the paint. It is tricky, but it can be done. The problem with this painting, Andrew, is that the paint is instantly soluble, with a solvent so mild it has scarcely any effect on the varnish."

As he listened, Andrew's brow wrinkled with concern — the likelihood that this painting could not be cleaned any further was becoming increasingly apparent.

Then Jerry delivered the clincher. "And look, Andrew. When I tried a cleaning test, the solvent immediately cut through the brown and revealed this," she said, pointing to the tiny speck of bright yellow now glinting from below.

Andrew became wary, hardly daring to reach the obvious conclusion. He asked slowly, "What do you think is going on, Jerry?"

"It looks as though there might be another painting under this one. I should warn you, however, that it might easily be no more important, and perhaps even less valuable, than the one you see now. Often the paintings underneath are incomplete because the painters gave up on the subject before it was finished. They scraped off as much of the paint as they could before reusing the canvas, so the 'painting' underneath is mostly destroyed.

"Having said that, I do find it strange that the paint below is so completely different from that above." Here she halted, hesitant to elaborate. She certainly had her suspicions, but her ideas were not yet fully formed. The clues did not add up, and she needed much more information before she was willing to plunge ahead with any coherent theory.

"Can you uncover more of the painting below?" he asked, now hoping his client's investment could be retrieved.

"Yes," she answered, "it's all too easy to get rid of the painting we are seeing now, but we need a better idea of what is underneath before we decide to sacrifice this painting for the one below."

"Information is usually expensive," he said with a smile, waiting to hear how much more this piece was going to cost.

"I'll need an x-ray. Fortunately this is not a large painting, so it won't take a lot of films to get the complete image," said Jerry, thinking out loud. "I can do cross-sections, but the medium and pigment analyses could be expensive. Shall I do an estimate?"

"Yes, please. The owner won't be happy with what we've got now. He paid a low price for a seventeenth-century contemporary of van Ruisdael, but that's still a rather high price for a nineteenth-century copy. Let's see what else you can find out."

Jerry told Andrew about her upcoming trip to London and her plans to talk to her old professor, Ben Johnson, about the painting. When she saw him out the door she realized he was still wearing his beautiful coat. She had never even offered to take it when he arrived. I really am distracted today, she thought. Looking down at her slim black trousers, dotted here and there with bits of Tony's tabby coat and Alvin's stark white, she frowned and got out her trusty sticky-roller.

"What is it about the wealthy, Tony?" she said as he reappeared now that Andrew had gone. "Did you ever notice that they never have cat hairs on their clothes? They don't even have lint! How do you think they do it? Is there some exclusive store somewhere that sells lint-resistant outfits? I guess I'm far too linty ever to be rich," she said happily, bending down to scoop Tony into her arms for a hug. Tony actually hated hugs, but he tried to endure the onslaught with grace. When he was allowed his freedom, Jerry had to pull out the sticky-roller once more, since in that one short encounter, he had managed to transfer a good deal of his coat onto her black sweater. "I swear he practices projectile shedding," she muttered to Alvin, who had also surfaced and had been watching the entire performance from a dignified distance.

Chapter 3

JERRY EMERGED FROM PADDINGTON STATION, where the shuttle train from Heathrow had deposited her, and took a deep breath of early morning London air: a potent mix of gasoline exhaust, garbage, and lingering unidentifiable but vaguely human odours. It was not entirely pleasant but brought back vivid memories of living in London, the most exciting and rich time of her entire life. The smell of London was the smell of being in the centre of, well, everything!

First order of business, she thought, was to get in the taxi queue, get to the hotel, and slip into bed for a few hours. She knew better than to attempt anything more demanding after her night flight from Toronto. She felt dishevelled, stressed, and even more linty than usual. Her best black slacks still bore vestiges of Alvin and Tony, now augmented by various fluffy additions from the cheap synthetic airline blanket.

The hotel was dreary, one of those huge 1960s buildings with mean cubbyholes for rooms. The TV seemed strangely outsized, until she realized that it was the miniaturization of all the room's contents that made it appear so large. She surveyed the narrow single mattress, "More like a cot than a bed. Oh, well, who cares, at least the sheets are clean," she said out loud, then climbed in gratefully to sleep off the flight.

Waking about six hours later, confused and groggy, she pulled herself out of bed and into the shower. She was meeting her old friend Patricia for dinner, an evening she had been looking forward to ever since she had been invited to London for the interview.

Jerry found her already seated at the smart restaurant in St. Martin's Lane where they had made a reservation. Patricia, also small and slender, currently had short cropped hair dyed pure white with dark roots. Fifties-style glasses with heavy dark rims completed her look. She was wearing the requisite black. Practically everyone in London of a certain age wore black. Welcoming the opportunity to give her friend a kiss on the cheek and a warm hug, Jerry thought how rare it was in Canada to show such affection for a friend. Still, remembering the satisfying little hug goodbye that she and Carol exchanged as she had left, she realized that people were becoming more demonstrative these days. I must be very hard up to count every hug I get from my friends, Jerry said ruefully to herself as she sat down at the table.

Her evening with Patricia was as delightful as Jerry had anticipated. Patricia knew all the latest London restoration gossip. The biggest news was a discovery of what had now been confirmed to be an authentic Gainsborough. Heavily overpainted, it had been taken to one of the top private studios. After the painstaking removal of a stubborn layer of old oil-based overpaint, the fresh and lively brushwork of Gainsborough had emerged. Of course all the restorers in the studio had known about its potential attribution, but no one was saying anything until the experts had been called in and the find was made public.

"Did James do the pigment and medium analysis?" asked Jerry. James was a prominent conservation scientist who was regularly called upon when any contentious or new attribution arose.

"Well, actually," Patricia began, looking uncomfortable, "he was only asked to do the pigment analysis."

"But what about the medium? Who did that?" Jerry asked, a little astonished.

"No one. Sir Alfred Wentworth-wet-bottom decreed it would not be necessary," responded Patricia. Jerry smiled at Patricia's facetious reference to the ever-unpopular art historian who, most restorers felt, had risen well above his abilities.

"I'm amazed they would overlook that. It's not that difficult to find 'authentic' pigments to forge a painting, but the medium is a much tougher proposition, isn't it? A fresh oil could never be made to look and act old enough; it would have to be doctored to get the effect of age. Surely they can't be a hundred-percent certain without medium analysis," she said, troubled. "That Gainsborough must be worth millions."

Patricia agreed, but reminded her that there was still a long way to go before the old-boy network gave way to new blood. Only then would a thorough knowledge of artists' materials be on a par with connoisseurship. "Still," Patricia continued, "there's a whole new generation of art historians now who have been educated to appreciate the sophisticated level of science that can be applied to the discovery of forgeries and misattributions."

"Don't worry, Jerry," Patricia added, "the days of the old-farts are numbered."

After the bill was settled, Jerry was glad to call it a day and return to her hotel. Tomorrow was Thursday. It would be a long day if she was going to visit the Chelsea Institute of Art and prepare for the interview on Friday.

Chapter 4

JERRY WOKE TO PALE, EARLY SPRING SUNSHINE bravely trying to penetrate the dingy net curtains in her hotel window. It was ridiculously early but she got up anyway, eager to be out and to reacquaint herself with London. Breakfast was much better than her hotel's general atmosphere suggested. Fortified with bacon, eggs, sausage, and toast, she was ready to meet the day. The journey on the underground was short, and she arrived at the Chelsea Institute of Art's grand quarters in what seemed like no time at all. As she walked towards the entrance, she realized it wasn't open yet.

She found a small café just down the street and sat with a cup of tea, watching the regulars picking up their coffee on their way to work. Coffee in the morning, tea in the afternoon. She smiled, remembering how she'd been corrected for writing "coffee break" into the afternoon schedule for a day-seminar she had helped to organize while at the Chelsea Institute of Art. In the afternoon, it's a "tea break."

Her plan was to have a good look around the Chelsea's collection before her appointment with Professor Johnson. One of the reasons the restoration training program at the Chelsea was so highly regarded was its close relationship with the painting collection, one of the best in the country. During Jerry's two years as an intern, after her formal training in Canada, she had worked on a number of the Chelsea's fine paintings.

Jerry was pleased to have an excuse to visit her old professor. She loved his dry wit and kind manners. He was a perfect gentleman, endlessly tolerant as a teacher. He never revealed if he found her questions naive, but always led her to information in a way that made her feel she was discovering it herself. Most of all, he had taught her to think critically, to reason through problems, and to explore below the surface. He introduced her to a level of subtlety that she had not experienced before. He would be the very best person with whom to discuss the problem with the painting she was working on.

She had time for a good tour of the collection on display in the gallery, then found a security guard to take her to the paintings studio upstairs. She entered the long narrow room, where paintings were propped on easels in a row in front of the windows. At the other end, she could see the tall, spare figure of her professor. He looked up from the student he was talking to and smiled with genuine pleasure.

"Ah, Jerry. What a treat to have you visit us. I won't be a minute, have a seat in my office."

She squeezed into a chair in his dusty crowded office and surveyed the piles of papers and books. Everywhere she looked was evidence of too much to do and too little time. A Renoir on an easel by the window was in the process of being expertly "inpainted" to cover small spots of missing paint.

Finally Professor Johnson arrived and cleared a space to sit down at his desk. He wore his half-reading glasses well down on the edge of a long thin nose, and peered over them at her through large brown eyes. She always thought he looked like a caricature of the absent-minded professor. His clothes, once good quality, were creased and unkempt. The daily issues of life appeared to pass him by; he looked like he needed to be reminded to eat. When she was an intern at the Chelsea Institute of Art, she had joined the other students in speculation about whether he was gay. It was hard to tell; sex could easily be among the conventional preoccupations he failed to engage in. Despite his complete lack of connection to the ordinary, and perhaps because of it, Jerry felt a strong affection for him. After exchanging a few pleasantries, she brought out her photographs of the painting and explained the difficulty she was having with the soluble paint.

"There's one scenario that could explain what you've found," he said after he had studied the photographs closely. "It's an old bit of trickery that used to be practised, and perhaps still is, to get valuable paintings through customs. The original is entirely overpainted with another image, usually intended to make it appear to be a second-rate painting. The top image has to look reasonably old in order to match the age of the canvas. Because it's meant to be temporary, the overpaint is designed to be easily removed. That would explain the unusual solubility of your current painting. It appears that something interrupted the normal course of events and the overpaint was never removed, leaving the painting disguised as a nineteenth-century copy."

"That's fascinating," said Jerry, shaking her head at the idea of such a scam. It had never occurred to her. "It certainly makes sense of the solubility problem. But there's something else. When I removed the acrylic overpainting, I couldn't find any reason for it to be there. Usually there's some damage or drying cracks that are being covered up, but not in this case."

"That is strange," he agreed. "Let me have another look at the before-treatment photo," he said, reaching over to the pile of large-format photographs Jerry had brought. He studied the image with the acrylic overpaint, then ventured, "It could be simply that the overpaint is there to create compositional changes, that sky for example. It's changed the scene rather a lot, hasn't it? Still, it's such depressingly bad work ... who would want to spoil a nice little nineteenth-century copy with that?"

The meeting ended abruptly when someone came to remind Professor Johnson of another appointment. As he was leaving, he invited Jerry to look around the studio and chat with the students, but she decided to find some lunch and return to her hotel to prepare for her interview the next day.

When she arrived back at her hotel, there was a recorded message for her from the professor. He apologized for having to rush off, and said that he had been thinking more about her painting. He wanted her to check with Nick Brooks at the Charles Haverstock Institute in Cambridge, who specialized in historical painting techniques and materials. He would be able to rule out any possibility that nineteenth-century paint could exhibit that level of solubility. He left Nick's number before hanging up.

Jerry naturally knew of Nick Brooks; he was a prominent figure in the restoration world, regularly presenting important and learned papers at international conferences. She was intimidated at the thought of contacting him but knew that she must. She was beginning to realize that she might be faced with removing the nineteenth-century painting. Such an important undertaking could not be done unless she could justify the loss of this painting to recover another. She immediately called to make an appointment.

Nick Brooks was very pleasant on the phone and expressed interest in her problem painting. He suggested that she come to Cambridge Friday afternoon. She agreed, knowing she would have ample time after her interview at the South Kensington Museum in the morning, to get up to Cambridge for a four o'clock meeting with Nick.

Her agenda arranged, she sat on the edge of the bed. "Now," she muttered to herself, "I have time to get *really* nervous about tomorrow's interview."

Chapter 5

FRIDAY MORNING THE INTERVIEW BOARD at the South
Kensington Museum convened to review the candidates' files
one last time before the interviews began. The panel included five
people: the head of the conservation department, the head of the
paintings studio, a senior restorer, the head of personnel, and one
of the senior conservation scientists. The head of conservation
welcomed them, and asked if they had all the information they
needed about the six applicants.

"Actually, although I'm sure that I've met them all at one time
or another," said the senior conservation scientist, "I'm having
trouble sorting them out. Which one is Jerry McPherson? Is she
the one that looks like Audrey Hepburn — you know, slender and
vaguely fragile?"

"Honestly, Bruce," said the head of personnel, "*all* the
women in restoration look like Audrey Hepburn, haven't you
noticed? It must be some kind of prerequisite."

Everyone smiled, then got down to work deciding the order
of questioning.

Jerry was interviewed third, giving her enough time to get
thoroughly rattled before she was invited in. She had chosen a tailored suit, its creamy-beige colour intended to disguise any errant
evidence of Tony and Alvin. She was determined to appear as
cool and confident as possible. Lint and assorted cat hairs would
not be part of her professional image that morning.

What the interviewers saw, as she entered the room, was a
slender young woman in her late twenties, medium height, and
fine-boned. They were impressed with the depth of her knowledge, and especially her understanding of the scientific principles
behind the treatment options open to a restorer. This was where

her particular training gave her an advantage. Many of the European programs concentrated on the materials, techniques, and practical skills. Science was not always heavily emphasized, so Jerry's background, a happy blend of both the North American system and the British, put her in a strong position. Her portfolio was equally impressive; she had successfully carried out a number of demanding and difficult treatments, and her skills at inpainting met the highest standards.

Afterwards, as she was leaving the museum, Jerry went over the interview in her mind and decided that it had gone well. Most of the panel had seemed open and receptive, even enthusiastic about her work. There was only one exception: the senior paintings restorer — she had been decidedly cool. Too bad, because she would probably be the person Jerry reported to. That could be a bit tricky.

Jerry had just enough time to grab a sandwich from a stall in King's Cross Station before she caught the train to Cambridge. She was grateful for the opportunity to do nothing but sit and look out the window for the hour-and-a-half train ride. She needed to unwind and collect herself before meeting Nick. She was sorry she hadn't had time to change out of her suit and into something more comfortable; she would have been much happier in a baggy sweater and slacks.

Nick had suggested they meet at the Fitzwilliam Museum on Trumpington Street, which was a straightforward taxi ride from the train station. He would normally be at the Charles Haverstock, but it was situated outside of Cambridge in the countryside, difficult to get to without a car. He told her he had some work to do at the Fitzwilliam, so it would be easy enough for him to be there instead.

In the taxi from the station, she was flooded with lovely memories of her stay in Cambridge when she was finishing her training in England. It was widely recognized that the two-year master's program in paintings conservation she had completed in Canada was only the beginning of professional training. Internships were necessary to become proficient in the practical side of restoration, and for Jerry, the ideal was to go to England. After her two years in the Chelsea Institute of Art's conservation department, she had spent several months at the Charles Haverstock on contract to assist in the restoration of a very large eighteenth-century painting. Part of the university, the Institute had been the grand country home of Sir Charles Haverstock before he bequeathed it to the university and it was converted into a restoration studio and training centre. A small but dedicated staff taught students to restore paintings, while outside the huge glass windows, the grounds and the English countryside beyond provided a beautiful and ageless setting.

Nick had been outside chatting with Peter Brown, one of the curators at the Fitzwilliam when Jerry's taxi drew up at the entrance. Peter recognized her and pointed her out.

"*That's* Jerry McPherson?" Nick blurted out. "I thought I'd met her before. I pictured her as one of those countless young women in black who are always milling around at gallery openings."

"Surprised at you, Nick. Thought you always had an eye for beauty," smiled Peter. "Now there's a young woman I would not be likely to forget."

"Hi, Peter, how nice to see you again," Jerry exclaimed happily as she shook hands with him. Peter gave her a quick peck on the cheek then introduced Nick, before excusing himself and disappearing into the museum.

"Shall we go and find a cup of tea somewhere?" Nick suggested as they shook hands. Jerry felt uncomfortable in her smart suit as she eyed his well-worn jeans and linen shirt under an old sweater. She felt overdressed and cursed her uncomfortable but stylish shoes as she and Nick made their way to a small café not far from the museum.

Once installed in a corner booth, Nick leaned forward to say, "I made a quick search in my database for any recipes that would have left the paint particularly sensitive to mild solvents while still having cracks such as you described to me on the phone." He continued, "There was precious little to indicate what could leave a nineteenth-century paint in that condition."

Jerry got out her photographs and passed them over. As Nick examined them, she sat and studied him. Up close and away from the podium, he was even more attractive than he appeared in his public lectures. His thick dark hair had the kind of tumbling rolling curls that every straight-haired person desperately wanted. His build is pretty bloody ideal, too, she thought, surveying the broad shoulders and easy way he relaxed in the booth across from her, while he frowned at the photographs. Rumours were always flying about him and who might be the woman he was most recently involved with. She was trying hard to remember the latest she had heard.

"I find the crack pattern on the paint rather odd," Nick said after a few minutes. "It's the kind of cracking one associates with old underbound paint. With a surface like this, the paint would ordinarily be extremely hard, and not at all sensitive to solvents. The only time I've seen paint with cracking something like this, that was still quite soluble, was when I was experimenting with mastic varnish. I added a very high proportion of it to fresh oil paint, which I made myself. The paint cracked within twenty-four hours, and the overload of mastic left it very sensitive to solvents."

"But," interrupted Jerry, "if the paint cracked in such a short time, wouldn't the artist have seen that and stopped using the mastic varnish?"

"I would think so, for anyone wanting to create a viable painting. However, if, as Ben Johnson suggested, this painting was meant as a cover for something underneath, then it was intended to look 'old,' so cracks and easy solubility were just what was wanted."

"That means the paint we are seeing now, which looks like a nineteenth-century copy, could actually have been put on at any time. It could even have been done in the twentieth century," reasoned Jerry.

"That's quite right. I think you need to find out more about what's under this painting. I have a feeling it will prove very interesting," he said, sitting back and stretching.

Throughout the meeting, there had been a slight *frisson* in the air. Jerry did not exactly feel uncomfortable, but she was not completely relaxed either. When Nick suggested that they go somewhere to find a bite to eat before she went back to London, she was torn. He was very attractive and interesting, but what would she be getting herself into? He must be in his early thirties. Surely he's involved with someone, she was thinking when she realized he was waiting for her answer. To her surprise, she heard herself saying, "That would be lovely, Nick. I'd enjoy that."

As soon as the words were out of her mouth, she gave herself a mental shaking. You idiot, he's probably bloody married with five children!

Despite her earlier misgivings, as the good wine and conversation flowed, she gave in to the warmth of the atmosphere in the little restaurant and to his easy charm. He regaled her with stories of the fakes and misattributions he had worked on. His knowledge of the intricacies of materials was truly remarkable. The time flew by, and suddenly she realized that she was in danger of missing the last train to London.

"Why don't you stay over? Tomorrow I could show you some of the paint samples I've been working on. You might see some similarities to the painting you have," said Nick when she pointed out the time.

She felt a lurch in her stomach as soon as he made the suggestion. Was she the proverbial fly getting caught in a well-spun web?

Sensing her reaction, Nick quickly said, "Um, I meant the invitation in an entirely friendly way." He continued, stammering, "That is, I didn't mean ... Oh hell, I have made a bit of an ass of myself," he trailed off lamely. Jerry relaxed, seeing his evident embarrassment. She gave him a brilliant smile, which had the opposite effect than intended. Now she'd just graduated from beautiful to gorgeous. Keen to assert his honourable intentions, which actually hadn't been all that honourable, he tried to salvage the situation, "Look, Jerry," he said earnestly, "I have quite a large flat here in Cambridge with an extra bedroom. You're welcome to be my guest."

It *was* late and she *was* exhausted. The idea of climbing into any bed at all that happened to be close by rather than taking the train back down to London was intensely attractive. At that moment, even more attractive than Nick himself. So she agreed. A short walk later, they were standing outside the door to Nick's flat. Too late to reconsider, Jerry decided she would just have to trust her instinct and not worry about spending the night at the home of a man she'd met only hours before. She took a deep breath to quell the nervousness she was beginning to feel.

As he opened the door, Nick, again his normal confident self, said with a smile, "I didn't mention that we'll have a chaperone." A large black streak of something with fur hurled itself at them.

"Minou hates being left alone," he said, bending down to pick up the cat. "And she tends to be the jealous type." Jerry found herself being sized up by two very large yellow eyes set in a pitch-black furry face.

Chapter 6

TRUE TO HIS WORD, NICK was a perfect gentleman. He brought her fresh towels, and a newly laundered T-shirt to sleep in, then wished her goodnight at the door of the guest room. Not even a peck on the cheek, she thought as she got into the bed, her face freshly scrubbed and teeth cleaned with a new brush left for her in the bathroom. Now, the danger to her honour past, she felt oddly disappointed. He probably thinks I'm not his type, she sighed, then rolled over and fell instantly asleep.

The next morning she felt like a new person. The interview behind her and with new information about her problem painting, she greeted the day with pleasure. Nick had found her a pair of old jeans that didn't fall down, a fresh T-shirt, and a pullover. Out of her designer suit, she looked much younger.

It was just warm enough to sit outside and have breakfast in the garden. A heavy teak table and matching chairs sat on a mouldy slate patio. The garden was very large, enclosed by high walls, the old bricks covered in vines. Although it was only March, roses climbed the walls and spilled out of the raised flower beds that ran around the perimeter. Several more beds of flowering shrubs and more roses held in check by a low course of bricks created small islands in the green well-tended lawn. Jerry wondered when Nick ever found the time to maintain such a lovely spot. She caught him scrutinizing her from across the breakfast table and immediately felt self-conscious. Did he find her attractive, or was he disappointed when he saw her in casual clothes; out of the armour of her interview suit?

Minou, extremely wary of Jerry, sat watching her as well, reluctant to get any closer than the door to the kitchen — which was a good twenty feet from the patio where she and Nick sat.

Despite the rather stony silence emanating from Minou's direction, Jerry attempted polite conversation: it would be too rude not to acknowledge the obvious mistress of the house.

She and Nick had a full day together, which she found very useful for her work. He took her around the Fitzwilliam Museum collection, then they drove out to the Charles Haverstock for the promised inspection of his historical paint reconstructions. They walked across the gravel parking lot and as they entered from a side door, she smelled the slight institutional fug of indoor air and years of use, a familiar mixture that took her back instantly to previous visits. Many of the furnishings and decorations in the house had been left in their original state when it was converted to a series of restoration studios. As a result, the décor had a decidedly eccentric air — the photocopy machine stood in a large hallway surrounded by once expensive and rather garish wallpaper better suited to a private home. In the kitchen the huge Aga stove supplied constant heat (if you were near enough to it). Lunch had usually been a communal affair, a chance for all the people working in the house to gather in one place and share cheese and bread. Occasionally someone would prepare a large stew or soup. For such a grand house, the kitchen was not very large, so everyone crammed around the table in an assortment of unmatched chairs. The living room, with its original fixtures and chandeliers, was used as a library and sometime lecture hall; students and staff would sit in comfort in deep plush sofas while they read or took notes. It was an expansive room with a high ceiling. As she entered, the verdant countryside waved back at her through distortions in the original glass of the windows that ran down the right wall. Jerry gazed out at the garden, remembering that, when the weather was sunny and warm, tea breaks were held outside. Then the warmth would seep into Jerry's bones, and she would be loathe to leave the idyllic countryside to return to the constant chill of the house's interior. But no one else was around to share a cup of tea, not on a Saturday. During the week the students and staff filled the house, but on the weekends it was often empty.

She wandered through the studios to see the paintings being worked on, and admired the progress being made on a very old piece that had been badly restored in the past but was recovering well under the careful ministrations of the staff. Nick's paint samples were fascinating. Some did look rather like her painting, in particular the one with an excess of mastic varnish that he had spoken about the night before. The cracking was indeed similar. There was a lot to see. He explained how he had prepared the paint samples by grinding pigments and oil together by hand, just as they would have in the past. The contrast between Nick's hand-ground paints and the modern paints squeezed from a tube was extreme. His showed a range of flow properties that one could not hope to find in modern commercial paint. No wonder the textures and surfaces of old master paintings appeared so different from one another and from modern works.

Jerry got the train to London around four in the afternoon, after stopping off at Nick's place to change back into her suit. At the station, he gave her a quick kiss on the cheek and squeezed her hand as she left him. They promised to keep in touch, and, as she sank into her seat, she basked in the afterglow of the lovely time she had had in his company. Just don't go getting any ideas, she warned herself sternly as the train pulled away. He lives on another continent, and you still don't know how single he is.

Jerry spent what was left of Saturday holed up in her hotel room watching the BBC and packing her bag for the trip back to Toronto the next day. She knew a lot of people she could have called, but she preferred to be on her own. Being by herself meant she could go over what she'd seen, burning in the images from the day, developing them like a series of photographs. She wanted to be able to recall those paint surfaces, the subtle differences between them, the pattern of the cracks. But it wasn't only the paint: she found herself replaying scenes with Nick — the way he looked at her across the breakfast table in the morning, how it felt to stand beside him in the upstairs studio while he was showing her the samples. She gave herself a shake. Stick to business, don't go there. He lives too far away, and the way he made her feel was dangerous. She didn't need the aggravation.

Chapter 7

SUNDAY MORNING, JERRY ARRIVED AT THE AIRPORT with plenty of time to spare. She liked to check in early so she could spend extra time in the bookshops, especially at Heathrow where she could find books that were not necessarily available in Canada. On this occasion, however, she had far more time on her hands than she had planned: her departure was delayed, at first by three hours. By the time she finally boarded the plane, the delay had been longer than the flight would be.

Clearing Canadian customs was also slow, and she arrived home in the early evening, more travel-weary than usual. When the taxi dropped her off in front of her building, the street was dark and empty. During the day large trucks came and went, servicing the warehouses that lined her street. By early evening, it was always deserted. Carol thought Jerry was crazy to live in such isolation. But the landlord had offered Jerry a cut-rate rent for the space — the first in a series of lofts he had planned for the building. When the renovations were all completed, the rent would probably climb or the building sold and she would have to look elsewhere. In the meantime, the loft was well appointed, the space was fabulous, and she didn't mind living alone, as long as she didn't think about it too hard.

Tired and grateful to be standing in the hallway at last, Jerry turned the key to her door, imagining herself in bed with two warm felines. When she stepped inside, however, she found the apartment strangely empty. Normally Alvin and Tony would be swarming around her ankles, Alvin telling her in no uncertain terms what he thought of *this* absence and how aggrieved he was. But there was nothing, not a sound. Not a sign of either of them.

She began to feel pricklings of fear. Dropping her bags, she called out, "Alvin? Tony? Where are you!?"

In the living room she bent down and looked under the couch, then checked in the kitchen. No sign of them and no note from Carol, either. Now truly alarmed, she walked into the bedroom and tried calling them in a softer voice. She checked under the bed and in the closet. Just as she was about to leave the bedroom, she heard a tiny rasping meow.

"Alvin?" she cried. "Tony? Where are you!?" She heard something again, this time from behind the large wicker laundry basket. She pulled the basket away from the wall. There, huddled together in a very small space, were two very frightened cats.

"What happened?" Jerry asked softly, bending down to stroke them.

"Jerry? Is that you in there?" Carol stood in the doorway with a large uniformed police officer behind her looking rather grim.

She stood up and gave Carol a quick hug. "I was so worried! The cats were hiding and they seem upset, what happened?" Then, as she caught sight of the police offficer, she cried out in horror, "Oh, my god, the painting!?"

"Don't worry, it's all right. It's just where you left it. But there was a break-in. While I was here. I must have scared them away. I've been down at the police station. This officer kindly offered to come back with me to make sure it was safe." Jerry looked over at the officer and managed a wan smile. He nodded, and asked if he might look around.

As they sat on the bed together, Carol explained that while she was waiting for Jerry, she felt one of her headaches coming on and had been lying down in the semi-darkness in the bedroom. Suddenly, Alvin and Tony slithered into the room and made for the laundry basket. "It was amazing, for two creatures normally at war they moved like one, keeping as close together as possible. Clearly something had frightened them," she continued. "I turned on the light and just as I got to the bedroom door, I saw the door to the loft closing. It scared the hell out of me, let me tell you."

Carol had phoned the police, then looked around to see if anything was missing. She shrugged. "Everything looked fine. I guess they'd just arrived and when they saw the light come on they took off."

"But how could they get the door open? What about the chains? That door is supposed to be impenetrable," said Jerry, perplexed.

Carol looked a bit sheepish; she knew how Jerry felt about security with the loft being in an industrial area rather than a friendly neighbourhood. "I didn't have the chains on. I thought you'd be home any minute."

The officer appeared at the bedroom door. He hadn't found any clues. There was no sign of a forced entry, so the lock might have been picked. He said he would check around outside before he left. They saw him to the door and thanked him for coming.

Jerry went back to the bedroom to see Alvin and Tony, who were now looking a little embarrassed. "Come on, guys, you deserve a big treat tonight," she said warmly, and reached over to the bedside table for a bag of cat treats. As she shook the dried food out onto the floor, Alvin, then Tony, uncurled themselves and ventured warily out of their hiding place. She stroked them both fondly as they ate, then she joined Carol who was making tea in the kitchen. "Couldn't we have something stronger?" she asked. "No wine in the fridge?"

"Yes of course, how silly of me," said Carol as she got out the wine. "I was in tea-for-emergencies mode. I forgot about fortifications."

It took a while for them to unwind. They sat together on the couch in the living room, working their way through the bottle of wine and speculating on the identity of the intruders. Jerry filled in Carol on her trip: the interview, Professor Johnson's thoughts on the painting, and, of course, Nick. She was glad to share her impressions of Nick with Carol. She was all the family Jerry had now that her parents were gone. It was the same for Carol, neither had brothers or sisters and Carol's parents had died not long after Jerry's. By the time the wine bottle was empty, they were ready to sleep. Carol opted for the couch, not wanting to leave her friend alone in the loft just yet.

The next morning, Carol left early for her own apartment to get dressed for work. Jerry phoned around to find a locksmith who could change her lock as soon as possible, hopefully this time for something unpickable. She spent the rest of the morning getting cost estimates for x-raying the painting and the pigment analysis. With the information in hand, she typed up a formal estimate of the total, her time included, and faxed it to Andrew.

By the afternoon, the locksmith having come and gone, and her immediate business taken care of, Jerry felt restless. She still had work to do on another painting, which was a simple case of varnish removal. She knew that she should get started on it, but the weather outside was sunny and bright. Instead she decided to take Alvin and Tony out for a walk to their favourite spot in the Moore Park Ravine, which ran off the Don Valley. Toronto's ravines, deep valleys cut by a network of creeks and streams that ran down to Lake Ontario, were one of Jerry's favourite features of the city. They all sheltered huge old trees and abundant wildlife.

Alvin had been introduced to car rides and walks in the ravine when he was a kitten; for him it was perfectly natural. Tony, who was well over a year old when he showed up on Jerry's fire escape under her bedroom window last spring, had been quick to learn the ropes from Alvin. They started out near the footbridge that crossed the north end of Moore Park Ravine. For their walks, Jerry always chose the middle of the morning or mid-afternoon when they were less likely to run into joggers using the Belt Line trail. As for cyclists, the cats could easily hear the sound of the tires crunching on the stone path and had ample time to hide while the bikes approached then whizzed by. Most of the time, however, they had the pathway to themselves, especially now in early spring when the days were still cool and the trees bare.

A walk "with" the cats was always entertaining. Their outing on this day followed the usual pattern. As she walked along, Tony and Alvin disappeared into the bushes by the side of the path, and reappeared, sometimes ahead of her, sometimes far behind. When they had fallen behind for a time, she heard the pounding of cat paws through the ground-cover of leaves as first one, then the other, came running up from behind, only to shoot past and back into the woods. Catching up must not be too obvious. Each cat was obliged to run on past, lest Jerry think that they were keeping pace with her. When it was time to go, Jerry climbed back up to the street, opened the passenger door of her car, and whistled. All pretense of independence was dropped; Alvin and Tony emerged from the woods and jumped in eagerly.

When she arrived back home, Andrew's fax was waiting in the machine, authorizing her to go ahead with the next stage of investigation into the painting.

Chapter 8

A FEW DAYS AFTER GETTING THE GO-AHEAD FROM ANDREW, Jerry was peering down through a microscope at a sample from the painting. She was in the conservation laboratory at the art gallery. The staff were happy to let her use their equipment, as long as she replaced supplies needed to prepare the paint sample for examination. They enjoyed visits with Jerry and looked forward to hearing what she was working on. Jerry was part of a close-knit circle of paintings restorers in Canada who shared ideas freely among themselves.

Her sample consisted of a tiny fragment of paint, which she had sliced off the painting at the edge of a crack using a surgical scalpel. Cutting through the paint down to the preparation layer was not always easy. Very old paint tended to crumble, and she needed a piece with all the layers of the painting intact. Fortunately she was able to cut into this paint relatively easily, managing to gather samples from six different areas of the painting. Such cross-sections were usually barely visible to the eye, but could contain a wealth of information about the layers of paint present, and the pigments used.

In order to manipulate such small specks of paint, Jerry had to encase each sample in its own block of plastic resin. She half-filled tiny moulds with liquid plastic. When it was almost hard, she put a paint sample in the centre of each mould and positioned it with the point of a needle. She then poured more plastic on top. Several hours later, when the plastic was cured, she cut the blocks in half so that the tiny speck of paint sat at the surface. The surface was then polished using a series of fine abrasives. After that it was relatively easy to position each sample in the microscope. At very high magnification, they looked like slices from a layer cake.

The microscope she was using allowed her to look at the paint sample under ultraviolet light as well as normal light. Under ultraviolet light, she could see the varnish layer more clearly, because the resin in the varnish fluoresced. Resin in the paint layer would also glow brightly, but oil alone would not.

Under normal light, the first cross-section looked ordinary. The uppermost layer was varnish, below that she could see a thick brown layer belonging to the landscape. The next layer, also quite thick, was varnish. Underneath that was another set of paint layers that interested Jerry the most. There were at least three layers, with the preparation, or ground, at the bottom. The pigments in these layers were completely different than in the brown paint above. Whereas the brown paint pigments were uniformly small, those in the layers below were coarse and showed a broad range in shapes and sizes. The colours were astonishingly brilliant: red, blue, and yellow flashed before her eyes. This paint was gorgeous. Jerry methodically studied each of the six cross-sections and found the same series of layers in each. When she changed to ultraviolet light, the paint samples no longer seemed ordinary: the brown paint on top glowed brightly, confirming her earlier suspicion that it would contain a high proportion of resin.

Something about the original paint was puzzling her a little. She asked one of the gallery's restorers to come and have a look.

"What do you think about this, Nancy?" she asked, as her colleague adjusted the eyepieces and focus to study the sample. "You can see that the top layer is very different from the paint below, and it's fluorescing like crazy. But what about the fluorescence in the original paint, don't you find that odd?"

"Hard to say," Nancy replied. "I don't think it's all that different than what we usually see for oil paintings. Maybe it's the way the microscope is set up. They do vary. How things appear depends a lot on the ultraviolet wave-length used and on the fluorescence from the casting resin holding the paint sample. Depends on what you're used to. Gosh, those colours are beautiful under that brown layer, aren't they?"

Chapter 9

JERRY CALLED ANDREW WHEN SHE HAD ASSEMBLED all the information on the painting: the scanning electron microscope results, the x-rays, and her own observations on the cross-sections. Now that she felt more confident about her interpretation of the layers, she was excited about what she had to present. This was turning out to be the most interesting piece she had ever worked on.

Andrew arrived at the loft early in the afternoon. This time she remembered to take his coat and to offer him coffee. As usual, Alvin and Tony had disappeared by the time he came in. They were careful about strangers, but seemed to make themselves especially scarce whenever he arrived. He shrugged out of his coat and declined the coffee. "Not now, I'm anxious to see what you have for me."

Jerry started with the most interesting first: the x-rays. Because the individual x-ray films were smaller than the painting, the radiographer had taken many separate shots. Each film depicted only part of the scene, but when they were overlapped on the light-box mounted on her studio wall, it was possible to view everything at once.

"This is fabulous!" said Andrew with excitement. "There's almost no interference from the paint on top — I can see three female figures, in what appears to be a landscape. There don't seem to be any large areas of damage. It looks like a complete painting!" His handsome face was far more animated than usual as he paced back and forth in front of the images. Jerry stood quietly, her arms crossed in front of her, and grinned.

"It gets better," she said after Andrew had had a good look at the x-rays. She led him over to the table where she had laid out the results of the pigment analyses and the photographs she had taken through the microscope of the paint cross-sections.

She picked up a black-and-white photograph of a cross-section taken under the scanning electron microscope. This gave them a vastly greater magnification than one could get under an ordinary light microscope; the electron microscope was also equipped with an energy dispersive x-ray detector, which identified the elements present in the paint. Jerry pointed to the white preparation layer at the bottom of the cross-section.

"See this area? That is mainly lead, probably from the lead white pigment in the ground. Of course that's typical, but look at this," she continued, pointing to a series of blotches in the bottom layers of paint. "The conservation scientist got a reading here for lead and for tin, which means we almost certainly have a lead-tin yellow pigment. And this," she said, pointing to another group of pigments, "is vermillion. He found loads of mercury and sulphur."

Lead-tin yellow was a pigment associated only with very old paintings. It was used frequently in Europe from as early as the 1300s, but after the middle of the eighteenth century it was no longer found, presumably falling out of use as other yellow pigments replaced it. The vermillion, also in use from very early times, did remain available, but the manufacturing process changed. In 1687 a new "wet process" method for making it was discovered, which could be easily differentiated from the earlier "dry process." The results from the analysis showed that the painter used dry process vermillion, another indication that this painting was old indeed.

Jerry watched Andrew as he frowned in concentration at the photographs. She broached the subject of medium analysis, which in her opinion, was necessary for confirmation that the landscape on top was a later addition. Because it was more expensive and time consuming than some of the other analyses, Andrew had rejected the idea from the outset and had asked her not to include it in her estimate. Now, with such promising indications that they had a very early painting, Jerry argued that medium analysis would be needed to verify that the nineteenth-century overpaint was not original. Andrew brushed her off, apparently unable to concentrate on the issue with the excitement of what the current analysis was revealing.

"Just go ahead and remove the painting on top, please Jerry. You have more than enough information to proceed," he said brusquely, irritation creeping into his voice. His mood had turned so quickly, Jerry was taken aback. This was quite a switch from his usual polished manners. She offered him a coffee, hoping to close the rift that had widened so suddenly between them. He refused, then abruptly walked over to the coat rack and prepared to leave, explaining that he must get in touch with the owner of the painting to tell him the good news. Almost as an afterthought, he turned to her. "Thanks very much, Jerry. You've done well. I'll call soon to hear how you're doing with the overpaint removal."

After the door closed behind him, she wandered the empty loft feeling let down. She had been very excited by the findings, and had been looking forward to sharing them with him. Something in his manner had really thrown her, and she wasn't entirely sure why.

"Alvin, Tony! You can come out now," she called. They appeared silently a few seconds later from the bedroom. As Jerry gave them cat treats and stroked them as they ate, she reflected on what had just happened. But she could not make sense of her unease.

The phone rang, and she rushed to pick it up, relieved by the distraction.

"Jerry, is that you?" said a deep voice with a British accent.

"Nick!" responded Jerry rather breathlessly. Her heart was pounding ridiculously hard and she was sure he could hear it.

"Listen, I'm in Ottawa, and ..."

"Ottawa! What on earth are you doing there?" she broke in.

"I'm on a courier trip to your National Gallery. I brought a painting from the Fitzwilliam for loan. I couldn't tell you before I left, of course, we're always sworn to secrecy about these trips. Mustn't alert the thieves, you know. I'd love to see you. How far is Toronto, can you come here for the weekend?"

"It's about five hours by car. Um, where are we," she said, thinking fast, "this is Thursday ... I could drive up tomorrow, I guess."

"I'm leaving from Ottawa on Monday morning. I could rent

a car and drive to Toronto if you would rather ..."

"No, it makes more sense for me to come there. I can spend Friday and Monday driving then we'd have two full days together. If you drove here it would eat into the time." She suddenly realized she was not doing a very good job at hiding her feelings. This is not exactly playing hard to get, she thought dryly to herself — so much for calm, cool, and collected.

But Nick had not sounded particularly casual either, she thought after they had hung up. They hadn't discussed where she would stay; apparently it was mutually assumed that she would share his room. She realized later that the possibility of either of them flying rather than driving had not entered her mind, but she knew that last-minute flights within Canada could be horrendously expensive, and as she thought it over she decided that Nick probably didn't have much more money to throw around than she did.

Pulled out of her abstraction by the sound of something falling off the counter in the kitchen, she went to investigate, not that she didn't already know full well what she would find. Sure enough, Tony was engaged in his favourite pastime of gently nudging anything moveable over the edge of the counter. She caught him as he was softly propelling a pen to the precipice, his ears cocked forward in anticipation of the delicious sound he was about to hear when it hit the floor.

"You're such an annoying cat," she chided as she bent down to retrieve the assortment he had already jettisoned: a tea bag, two forks, her necklace, the front-door key, and a corkscrew. "I don't remember leaving all these things on the counter," she murmured as she put them away. "And how did you get the key off its hook?" she asked as she hung it back up. "Practising a little telekenesis were you? Did you gather all these things up here just so you could enjoy knocking them down?"

❦

Carol agreed to look after Alvin and Tony while she was away. "But on one condition. This time they stay at my apartment," she insisted, still feeling uncomfortable about the attempted break-in.

Jerry agreed and said she would bring them over first thing the next morning on her way out of the city.

Jerry was looking forward to the drive. The highway was mostly straight and the driving at this time of year in good weather was relatively undemanding. She just had to get on the highway, drive for five hours, and get off. Simple. Not like trying to drive on the English motorways. There, every time she thought she was through with all the ramps and collector lanes and finally onto a straight-away where she could relax and sink into her own thoughts for a few hours, she would find herself faced with a new decision about whether to split off to the left or to the right. Then, seconds later she would be in another collector lane on her way to connect with yet another motorway. Driving long distances in England had nothing of the relaxing mind-numbing travel she was used to in Canada, where miles and miles of highway stretched across a landscape which appeared to be totally empty of people.

Still, if I had a choice, she thought to herself, I would trade the long unbroken miles in Canada for the thrill of being in England again. That reminded her, what about the position at the South Kensington Museum? It had been over three weeks since the interview, surely they should be getting in touch soon. But then she had not heard about the job in Toronto either, and that had been at least five weeks ago. It's difficult hovering between two futures like this, she thought as she got out her suitcase to begin packing for the weekend. Tony and Alvin, predictably, began to interfere with her preparations. Alvin kept jumping into the suitcase, lavishing his long pure-white cat hair over her fresh clothing, and Tony tried to trip her up at every opportunity as she moved between the suitcase on the bed and the closet.

"All right you two, I've had enough!" she announced as she took one cat after the other out of the suitcase for what seemed like the ninety-ninth time. "I am going to get *Alice*."

A short while later, Carol let herself into the loft.

"What are you doing with Alice?" she exclaimed when she saw the skeleton hanging in the doorway to Jerry's bedroom.

"Oh, um ... Hi, Carol. Alice is acting as a cat deterrent. I couldn't get Tony and Alvin to leave me alone while I was packing, so I put them in the kitchen and moved her here. They won't go near her. As long as she's in the doorway, they won't come into the room," said Jerry a little apologetically. Alice was, after all, Carol's skeleton, or rather Carol's family's skeleton. Alice had belonged to Carol's great-grandfather who had been a doctor. It had been normal practice in those days to keep a skeleton in the surgery. Alice had ended up with Carol's grandmother and when she died, Carol had offered Alice to Jerry who was taking classes in anatomical drawing.

"Isn't it illegal or something, to have human remains around?" Jerry had asked.

"I don't know."

"Well, shouldn't you give it to a museum or medical school?"

"I suppose, but I thought you might like her," Carol had answered.

"Why is it called Alice?"

"We have always called *her* Alice," replied Carol rather curtly, apparently considering Alice to be possibly one of the family.

The two had had a hilarious time moving Alice out of Carol's grandmother's basement, into Jerry's hatchback, and up to her studio in the loft. They had felt uneasy, convinced the police would somehow know they were transporting something suspicious. However, once Alice was in the studio, Jerry was glad to have taken the risk, if indeed there really had been a risk. She consulted Alice whenever she was working on a figure painting and needed to fill in missing detail; she had proved quite useful. Jerry was sorry that Carol had discovered her using Alice in a less conventional way. As she helped Jerry move the skeleton back to her regular spot in the studio beside the large metal solvent cupboard, Carol asked, "Why didn't you just close the bedroom door? Wouldn't that keep the cats out?"

"If I close the door on them they kick up a terrible fuss and start scratching and meowing outside. They drive me crazy." She continued, "Anyway, the light is much better in the bedroom with the door open. You don't want me packing any metameric mismatches, do you?" she joked.

She was referring to metamerism, one of the first lessons a restorer learned about colour matching. Some colours change significantly in different light conditions — blues and browns are especially prone to this. If inpainting colours were matched to the original paint in the wrong light conditions, the inpainting would show when the painting was hung in a gallery. The only sure way of avoiding the problem was to match colours in daylight, hence the need for a bank of windows in restoration studios. There were special colour-matching fluorescent lights available, but most restorers preferred to have access to natural light.

Alice had just been returned to her accustomed spot when the phone rang. It was Andrew wanting to know how she was getting along with the overpaint removal. Since he had only left a few hours ago, it seemed a bit much for him to be calling so soon. Jerry explained that she would begin early the next week.

"What do you think has gotten up his nose, Carol? Andrew is normally so understated and cool. He didn't sound at all pleased to hear I wasn't working on his painting *right this minute*. It's funny how fast he can switch from charming to rude these days. Do you think he's too young for male menopause?"

Chapter 10

JERRY HAD LEFT FOR OTTAWA LATER THAN PLANNED because Alvin and Tony had refused to co-operate, knowing that they were not about to go out for a walk in the ravine. It had taken ages to track them down and wrestle them into their carriers. Alvin had been especially exasperating. When she got him head first at the cage door, he somehow managed to fold himself up like an accordion: front feet planted firmly on the floor, with his backside sliding forward as she pushed, but no actual progress into the cage.

"Honestly, Alvin, you're defying the laws of physics. It's impossible for you to compress yourself like this, it can't be done!" she said through gritted teeth as she gave him another shove, and still his head went no further into the carrier. Finally, sensing that Jerry was truly determined, he suddenly flowed forward in one easy motion. "Bloody cats," she muttered as she closed the carrier door firmly.

Jerry arrived in Ottawa around three in the afternoon. The drive itself had been as pleasantly uneventful as she had anticipated, giving her lots of time to mull over the past weeks and the developments with the painting. She hadn't been at all nervous about seeing Nick again, that is, not up until the moment she got out of the car in front of the hotel.

What am I doing? she asked herself as she felt the butterflies starting in her stomach. This is completely mad. Then she caught sight of Nick and her legs turned to jelly. She started to panic, and thought, my whole body is going to fall apart any second, I think I have to ...

"Jerry!" Nick called, interrupting her now full-blown panic. He was over to her in seconds and swept her into an embrace that took the last bit of her breath away.

Later, lying in bed in Nick's arms, she snuggled deeper into his chest and murmured, "You must think I'm awfully easy. The truth is, I thought complete capitulation was the only way I would get to bed in time. Seeing you made my legs so weak, I thought I might faint."

"Oh, really?" said Nick amused. "You only made love to me because it was easier than fainting in the hotel lobby? I'm glad you're not a romantic, Jerry. You're obviously a thoroughly practical woman." He kissed her forehead tenderly and pulled her a little closer.

A few hours later they roused themselves enough to order room service and enjoy a delicious meal, wheeled in on a table covered with crisp white linen and gleaming silver. Nick had ordered champagne, to celebrate.

"Celebrate what?" asked Jerry, with a smile as she looked at him over her champagne flute.

"Your practicality, what else?" he smiled back.

❧

The next morning Jerry lay happily beside Nick and decided that she would let nothing spoil her mood or dampen her spirits. She was not going to think about Nick leaving Monday morning. Instead she would savour every moment they had together.

It took them forever to get out of the Lord Elgin Hotel; somehow they kept ending up back in bed. They finally dragged themselves out with the promise of a late lunch in the nearby market area. As they walked up Elgin Street towards the war memorial they could see the Gothic features of the Parliament buildings on the left and the fairy-tale turrets of the Château Laurier to their right: Ottawa's grand old hotel that used to sit across from the railway station. The railway lines had been ripped up long ago. Now the station building loomed sullenly beside the canal. They rounded the corner at the Château Laurier and descended stone steps close to the American Embassy. Dressed up as an elegant fortress, it appeared ready to withstand whatever madness might arise. In bureaucratic Ottawa, Jerry thought the building looked overdesigned; she found it hard to imagine a threat any more serious than a strongly worded memo. They continued past tall grey-stoned buildings, and found the old market itself, a long red-brick building stuffed with touristy shops.

The early spring air was fresh, but the sun had regained some of its strength over the past few weeks, so they searched for a restaurant with an outdoor terrace. They found a sunny spot on Clarence Street, just north of the market. There, a series of restaurant terraces competed with crowds of people for a small strip between the storefronts and the street. Plastic tables, chairs, and umbrellas crammed the sidewalk, the Saturday crowds squeezing by within touching distance. The wind was still chilly. Jerry and Nick huddled over their salads, feeling cold every time the clouds covered the sun.

Their conversation turned to the painting. Jerry filled Nick in on the results of the x-rays and analyses. He was excited about the pigments that had been found.

"This sounds very promising. Ben's idea of a second-rate painting covering something valuable could be correct. It will be very interesting to see what turns up as you take off the overpaint. I wish I could be there to watch," he said, as he casually picked up one of her hands and started to play with her fingers. Jerry was suddenly finding it very difficult to concentrate.

She really wanted to discuss the painting with him, but she was fighting a silly unreal feeling that she supposed was hormone-induced. It was making it very difficult for her to focus for more than a split-second on anything else but the smell, feel, and look of Nick. Nevertheless, she pulled herself together as much as she could and plunged ahead with her questions.

"Nick, what about the medium analysis? It's been bothering me that Andrew doesn't seem to want it done. Isn't it the only sure way of knowing that the overpaint is inconsistent and that it can be removed without any fear that it was added by the artist himself?"

"Sometimes it's the only certain way of establishing that a layer of paint is not by the hand of the artist. But of course that's only the case if analysis turns up some material anachronistic to the original."

"You mean, if one of the layers has a synthetic resin in it, something invented in the twentieth century, or some natural material that wasn't available when the original painting was made?"

"Yes, but often it's not that simple. Another painter may have changed it shortly after it was completed. There's a well-known case of a Constable where the owner had another artist paint over the sky because he thought Constable's looked unfinished. Since it was done within decades of the painting's completion, the new paint was completely consistent with the type of paint Constable used. Analysis would not be able to establish that the new paint was not his."

"Then how did they know?" she asked.

"There were records: letters between the owner and the artist who had redone the sky, accounts by contemporaries that it had happened. There was a lot of documentary evidence. And there was the painting itself. On close examination, one could see that the brushstrokes and the whole style of painting were quite different from Constable's. There was no attempt by the other artist to hide his own work, no effort to match Constable's style. With a bit of careful looking, it was obvious."

"So they removed the overpaint?"

"Yes, but only with great difficulty, because it was taking oil paint off of oil paint, so the solubility was very similar. It was mostly done mechanically — with a scalpel. Painstaking work, but well worth it in the end. Constable's own sky was vastly superior."

Nick paused to consider, then continued, "Discovering what is overpaint and what doesn't belong to the original painting can be complicated. As you know, artists will reuse old paintings they've had hanging about the studio, painting over their own work, sometimes decades later. And they will also change elements of their own compositions in completely finished paintings. I know of an instance where an owner brought a painting back to the artist for a minor repair, there was a small tear in the canvas, and he ended up with a freshly painted image because the artist no longer liked what he had done before. When artists repaint their own work, their own style has often developed and their repaints are not always sympathetic to their original composition. It certainly can get confusing, and usually pigment and medium analysis won't help. Though a close look at the cross-sections can sometimes sort out what's happened."

"If artists do change passages in their own paintings, no matter how many years later, isn't it difficult to justify taking off the changes?" asked Jerry.

"It's difficult," smiled Nick, who was clearly no longer concentrating on their conversation.

"Stop it, Nick!" she said when she saw the look in his eye. She did not want to succumb just yet and float off into the hormonal-ether before they had finished this discussion. She continued with some urgency, "I *need* to talk to you about this. It's really important. I have never been faced with the prospect of removing a whole painting from on top of another; I'm nervous about it. I want to be sure this is the right thing to do."

"Jerry, don't worry. From the evidence you've shown me, it's staringly obvious that the paint on top is not original. Nor is it from the same century as the paint below. I realize the pigments in the overpaint are not inconsistent because they are mainly earth pigments, which have existed since the beginning of time. However, the appearance of the paint, the small size of the pigment particles, and their uniformity are usually dead giveaways that the paint on top is relatively modern. I would not hesitate, myself. But, if it would make you feel better, I could have some medium analysis done. Maybe there will be something nice and inconsistent in that overpaint to reassure you."

Jerry's eyes lit up and she visibly relaxed. "Oh, Nick, I was hoping you might say that. Yes, please do have a look at the paint. I would appreciate that so much. But how long do you think it will take? Andrew is breathing down my neck about getting on with the paint removal."

"Once I have the sample I can take it to my colleague in the university science department at Cambridge. Roger is usually good about running samples quickly for me. I could have something back from him in a few days."

Jerry was rummaging around in her purse as he spoke, and produced three small glass vials in a plastic bag. "Here you are. I brought some samples, just in case you might offer. Do you think this is enough?" she asked as she handed them to him.

He held one of the vials and tapped it on the back of his finger nail to bring all of the tiny paint specks down to the bottom. The vial was funnel-shaped inside, so that the sample collected into a point at the base. The paint was mainly brown. Holding it up to the light, he asked, "Is this the overpaint?"

"If that is the vial marked one, it is — look on the base. There's also a sample from the original paint, in the vial marked two. I put a rather large cross-section from the whole painting into vial number three."

"Good. It looks like there's plenty of paint for analysis. Extraordinary, isn't it? Ten years ago it was impossible to learn anything about the medium with this tiny amount. I should be able to tell you something by the end of this week. Is that all right?"

This time it was Jerry who was no longer concentrating. Nick looked up from the samples and caught her smiling in a way that made it obvious she had given up on business for the time being. He laughed and leaned over to tousle her hair.

The rest of the weekend remained sunny and mild. Whenever Nick and Jerry ventured outside their hotel room and its oversized bed, they walked arm in arm, enjoying being together, oblivious to their location. Monday arrived all too soon. It was a sad parting, made especially difficult because there were no immediate plans for when they might see each other again. Nick's trip to Ottawa to courier the painting from the Fitzwilliam came up unexpectedly when the regular courier fell ill. There was a chance that he would be the one asked to accompany the painting back at the end of the exhibition because the museum liked to use the same courier for both the inward and outward journey. But that wouldn't be for another three months.

Despite the indefinite separation facing them, something about the way they were together made Jerry quite certain this was no isolated affair, but the beginning of an exploration that would continue. She was sure that Nick shared her view. She drove back to Toronto feeling rather numb and suspended. Her world had just taken a grand tilt. What was next did not concern her particularly. She felt rooted in the images of Nick she now carried in her mind and her thoughts were utterly absorbed in him.

Chapter 11

Jerry arrived back in Toronto late on Monday afternoon and went straight to Carol's to pick up the cats. Knowing Carol would still be at work, she used her key to her friend's apartment. Tony and Alvin were there to greet her, obviously overjoyed. "Glad to know that you two don't bear a grudge," she said, giving each a thorough hug. "I see you've forgiven me for leaving you. Thanks guys."

By the time she had put the cats into her car, a cold rain had begun to fall and it had turned unnaturally dark for the time of day. As she drove down the Don Valley Parkway, the rain was getting thicker and thicker, eventually turning into a mixture of sleet and rain. At least this might be the last snow for the year, she thought grimly. The streets in the city were black and wet, the sky deep grey. She pulled up in front of her building, finding a parking space close to the entrance. The old red-brick warehouse was dark except for security lights outside.

She carried Alvin and Tony easily up the three flights of stairs. Funny the way cats can change their weight at will, she mused as she remembered how intensely heavy they had been on the way down, just three days ago. Not only heavy, but there had been a peculiar dense silence emanating from their carriers, a tangible disapproving silence.

"Amazing little creatures, aren't you?" she said out loud, her voice echoing in the stairwell.

At the door, she set down their carriers and fumbled through her handbag for her key. As the door swung open, she crouched down to release the carrier doors. When she straightened, she was surprised to see both cats poking their noses out very cautiously, moving slowly and sniffing the air. "What's up with you two?" she said, puzzled. Normally they would have bounded out of their carriers in a second, eager to be back home.

Feeling on edge, Jerry stared into the dark apartment. She walked in and turned on the lights. Everything appeared to be in order. Suddenly it dawned on her. She stopped, squeezed her eyes shut for a second, and slowly turned to looked at the easel in the studio.

It was empty.

"Damn!" she breathed, her heart pounding in her throat. "This can't be happening." She rushed to the easel. Maybe I put the painting away, she thought wildly. No, she *had* left it there. Her eyes moved past the easel to the metal shutters that were rolled down over the windows. They looked tightly closed. They, and her microscope, had been the most expensive equipment she had had to buy when she set up her studio. She was still paying for them.

"Fat lot of good you did me!" she shouted at the shutters.

Jerry tried to pull herself together, to think what was next. "I must call Andrew, I must call the police."

Meanwhile Alvin and Tony were making a thorough inspection, carefully sniffing every corner. "Let me know if you find anything," she said as she started dialling. Andrew picked up after the first ring. He groaned when she told him the news, and said he would be over right away. Meanwhile, she called the police. Soon the loft was full of people. Andrew brought a reporter with him, explaining that he wanted to announce the theft in the papers, in hopes of flushing out the thieves as soon as possible. "Maybe we can catch them before the painting leaves the country," he said, a bit breathlessly, obviously caught up in all the excitement.

Among the police was Detective-Sergeant Wiens from the art fraud unit. He was the only person who seemed to know what to do; everyone else just hung around, or so it seemed to Jerry, who was trying to make coffee for what was now a crowd.

Detective-Sergeant Wiens agreed with Andrew that they should try to give the theft as much publicity as possible. It would alert the dealers, perhaps someone who knew something would phone in a lead. When he saw a photograph of the painting, he seemed a bit surprised.

"Forgive me for saying, but," he hesitated, "this painting looks pretty ordinary. I'm surprised it was the only thing taken. You didn't have any other, more important pieces here that are gone, too?" he asked.

Jerry assured him that it was the only thing missing. The portraits she was working on were still in the storage racks. Nothing else had been disturbed.

She gave the reporter a large black-and-white photograph of the painting taken after the acrylic overpaint had been removed. Andrew explained to him that it was a nineteenth-century copy of a painting by Jacob van Ruisdael, a famous seventeenth-century Dutch landscapist. He did not mention that there seemed to be something far more interesting underneath.

The reporter said he would submit his piece in time for the morning paper. Wiens gave him a number for readers to call if they had any information that might lead to the recovery of the painting. He requested that the article be given a prominent position. Then he turned to Jerry. "Sometimes we get lucky. However, we've had a very professional group working the city for the past six months. Your piece would not normally warrant this amount of attention," he added disparagingly, "but it may lead us to the thieves we're after."

Jerry was quite irritated by his manner. An art snob! Imagine a police officer pronouncing on the value of a painting, she thought to herself, studying him more closely. Wiens certainly did not fit the picture of an aesthete. He wore boring brown polyester trousers with a beige poly-cotton dress shirt tucked into a rather pudgy waist. His suit jacket looked like it must be the only one he had; on the hanger it probably still carried the imprint of his slouch. She would never have noticed him on the street, he was so ordinary. He was positively invisible — maybe that made him a good investigator, she thought reluctantly.

Carol arrived while the crowd was still hovering about the scene of the crime. "I just got your phone message. This is unbelievable," she said. "How did they get in? I thought your new lock was supposed to be impregnable."

Jerry sighed, "That's what the locksmith told me. He said it was virtually impossible to pick these locks and every key was registered. The police said it looked like a professional job. The metal doorchains were cut."

When everyone had finally left, Jerry sank onto her couch, completely drained. The drive from Ottawa had made it long day, and while she had spent most of the weekend in bed, she certainly hadn't gotten much sleep. Alvin jumped onto her lap, and soon Tony joined them by her side. She petted them automatically. Carol had offered to stay, or to have Jerry and the cats to her place. But she just wanted to be alone. Now that the painting was gone, she felt sure there would be no more break-ins. Jerry climbed into her comfortable bed and lay in the dark. She felt one cat, then another, land on top of the covers and curl up at her feet as she slipped into unconsciousness.

Tuesday, still numb and unable to respond to the shock of the theft, Jerry concentrated on removing varnish from one of the portraits. It was a nice, straightforward job. The varnish obligingly dissolved in a standard mixture of alcohol and another fast-evaporating solvent. As the paint emerged, its colours released from the dark yellow of the old varnish, the image sparkled.

Jerry moved through the day like a sleep walker. By late afternoon she was having trouble concentrating on her work, so she rented a video from the nearest corner store and sat curled up on the couch, unable to care whether the heroine escaped the clutches of an army of aliens or whether she would be absorbed into their species.

"I wouldn't mind being absorbed into another species right about now," she said lazily to Alvin as the movie ended. "I'm not feeling too hot about my own at the moment." Alvin murmured a half purr—half meow and butted his head against her hand, wanting her to stroke him.

The phone rang.

"Jerry, are you all right?" It was Nick, sounding worried. "I just read your email. How *are* you?"

"I'm fine. Thanks so much for calling. I'm just ... disappointed mainly. Hugely disappointed. I was really looking forward to working on that painting. And now it's vanished. Disappeared. I can't quite take it in."

"It's bizarre," he said, "very strange timing. Another couple of weeks and they would have stolen a completely different painting, maybe much more valuable. They probably have no idea what they have in their hands." As an afterthought he added, " I have the results from the medium analysis on your overpaint already. I dropped it off on my way home this morning, and Roger was kind enough to run the sample right away. He left me a message while I was sleeping off the flight. He found a lot of resin in it, as we suspected, and you're in luck: the resin is dammar. It wasn't introduced into the artists' market until 1827. Your overpaint cannot be any older than that."

"Great, Nick. So I can go ahead and remove it now, right?" she replied.

"Oh, I am sorry," he said, suddenly realizing the irony. "It must be terribly frustrating. Everything in place for you to proceed, and no painting!"

They talked on, eventually getting to the subject of their weekend together. Jerry felt awkward; she did not have the words to express the enormous changes being with Nick had touched off. She wanted so much to be with him, as close as humanly possible. "Maybe even closer," she joked, as she told him about the video with people being assimilated by aliens. "I wouldn't mind being absorbed by you," she said lightly. Nick laughed and rejoined that he was certainly finding himself absorbed by her. In fact, he was having trouble keeping his mind on anything else.

After they hung up, her earlier numbness was replaced by longing. She gave herself a shake. "Really, I would much rather be numb again, this is no fun at all," she said to Alvin. Fortunately she still had another movie to watch, that would get her through another few hours and then it would be late enough for the solace of her bed and the oblivion of sleep.

Carol called halfway through the second video. "Have you seen the newspaper story?" she asked excitedly.

"No, not yet. Is it okay?"

"Well, you've made a splash. The article on the robbery was in the first section of *The Star* this morning with a large photograph of the painting. And there was another article. They interviewed that guy who specializes in art fraud, and he referred to your painting, too."

"Good publicity for my business," said Jerry sarcastically. "Just think of all the new work I"ll get now that everyone knows about the great security here."

"Don't worry, it'll blow over in a few days. No one will remember."

Wednesday morning she was awakened by the phone. It was the Toronto museum informing her that the position had been awarded to another candidate.

She was taken aback. In the time between being interviewed for the job and now, so much had changed that she doubted she even wanted to stay in Toronto anymore. Still, she knew she was the best candidate for that position. It was incredible that they hadn't offered it to her.

Carol dropped by on her way home after work. The museum grapevine had reached her with the news that the position was filled, and she knew Jerry had not been chosen. She arrived with a cold bottle of Chablis, hoping she could cheer her up. She found Jerry rather philosophical about it, but still puzzled. As they discussed the chosen candidate and his singular lack of experience, it dawned on them both, at about the same time.

"That bloody break-in. They took one look at the newspaper article and decided I would be an embarrassment to them. I can just see the headlines they must have imagined: 'Museum hires restorer who lost valuable painting.'"

"It wasn't *that* valuable, Jerry," admonished Carol.

"No, not when it was stolen. But underneath that overpaint, who knows!"

Chapter 12

ON FRIDAY JERRY WAS WORKING QUIETLY IN HER STUDIO. The week had been tremendously draining for her. Most of the time when the phone rang, she just let it take a message, not wanting to speak to anyone. But when she heard Andrew's voice on the answering machine, she dropped what she was doing and picked up right away. He had a message from the police about the painting. He had to rush off for an important meeting, could she contact them to find out what it was about.

Jerry dialled the number Detective-Sergeant Wiens had given her. "This is Jerry McPherson. I'm phoning about the missing painting Detective-Sergeant Wiens is investigating. Is there any news?"

"Ah yes, Ms. McPherson. We've recovered a painting that appears to be the one that disappeared from your studio. Can you come down to identify it?"

"Oh, my god. Of course! Yes, right away! Where do I come?"

As she entered Wiens's office, she saw the painting sitting on a flimsy metal easel. It looked smaller and strangely incongruous, surrounded by his smudgy beige office walls. She sank into a chair, keeping her eyes fixed on it. When Wiens spoke, it was an effort to pull herself away to look at him.

"Ms. McPherson ...," he began.

She interrupted, "How did you find it? Where was it? Do you know who took it?"

Wiens leaned back in his chair and crossed his arms over his chest. "We received a locker key in a plain white envelope. It was on my desk this morning when I came in," he explained. "The key was from Union Station. One of my men checked it out.

"Of course I told him not to touch anything," he assured her, as he saw her eyebrows lift, old paintings were easily damaged by inexperienced handling. "I went down and got it myself."

"But isn't that strange, leaving it in a locker, at the *train* station? Why would someone do that? And why tell you?"

"It's not that unusual. If they didn't have a buyer lined up beforehand, they were probably counting on selling it locally. Thanks to the article in *The Star,* the painting became difficult to fence because everyone in the business was watching for it."

"But why make it so easy for you, why not just ditch it?"

"It became a liability for them, so they got rid of it by letting it be known where it could be found. They knew what they had, they didn't want it destroyed." He looked at Jerry slightly disapprovingly, as if she had missed something essential, then continued. "People who steal art are not always without *feelings,* Ms. McPherson. They usually respect what they have, you know, even if it belongs to someone else."

⁂

Carol, who had dropped in on Jerry during her lunch hour, stood in front of the painting where it sat once again on its wooden easel and listened to the description of her encounter with Detective-Sergeant Wiens. She burst out, "Honestly, he sounds like a complete nutter to me. Imagine saying that art thieves have 'feelings.' I think he's been working too hard, don't you?"

Jerry laughed and nodded her head. "But remember that case in Europe when Munch's famous painting *The Scream* was stolen? The thieves eventually told the police where to find it."

"But wasn't that politically motivated? They stole it to make a point about something," Carol replied.

Jerry agreed. Still she was beginning to develop a grudging respect for Wiens. Despite his lack of taste in clothes, he seemed to know his job, and because he was so unperturbed about the manner in which the painting had been returned, she decided it was probably not quite as strange as it seemed to her and Carol. Nevertheless, it felt a bit weird, having the painting back so soon and being so easy to find.

"Well, I'm not intending to look a gift horse in the mouth," said Jerry, her good humour restored. "I can barely wait to get started on it."

Andrew had been relieved when she told him the good news, but he didn't rush over to see the piece. Instead, once the news had sunk in, he urged Jerry to get on with the overpaint removal. This time she assured him she had no intention of working on anything else until it was finished.

After Carol left to go back to work, Jerry decided to get down to business. She left a message on Nick's machine telling him what had happened, then rolled up her sleeves, put on her black smock, and began measuring out the solvents she would need.

As she had anticipated, the nineteenth-century scene yielded easily to her solvent mixture. The paint dissolved away, turning the white solvent-soaked cotton swabs she was using to a dirty brown. Her movements became routine: as soon as the cotton was covered with paint, she would pull it off the stick and start over with a fresh piece, dipping it in the solvent and blotting off the excess before rolling it over the paint.

Jerry worked for about half an hour, then stood back to survey her progress. She had cleaned off a square about two inches in size, enough to reveal a rich deep yellow, part of the robe of one of the figures they had seen in the x-rays. Already she could see that the brushwork was sure and masterful. She started in again, working methodically and with care. She regularly checked the paint that she was uncovering under the stereomicroscope. She wanted to be sure that the newly recovered paint was not being damaged by her solvent. It didn't appear to be affected at all. The paint surface was still covered with a layer of varnish. It had a fine low luster, and the paint below appeared to be in excellent condition.

It took two or three swabs before she was down to the original surface, then another two to remove the residue of overpaint. Jerry saved the dirty swabs as she worked, a habit many restorers acquired. During varnish removal they were useful for comparing one part of the painting with another. The varnish residue should match no matter where it was taken from the painting. If the swabs took on a slightly reddish tinge while working over red paint, for example, that would indicate that the paint was being affected. For overpaint removal she was saving the swabs so that if there was any dispute about what she removed, the swabs could be analyzed.

She had been working intently, when her concentration was broken by the sound of something hard hitting the floor in the kitchen. Tony was up on the counter and a can of cat food was on the floor. At least he had the wherewithal to look guilty. She was about to begin a severe reprimand when she caught sight of the clock in the kitchen.

"Oh, Tony, you are a rotten old cat to get up on the counter again," she said gently, "but you're right, it's well past your dinner. I'm sorry, I completely lost track of the time."

Jerry took off her optivisor, the magnifying glasses on a head-band that allowed her to see the surface she was working on in more detail, and in a single lithe movement, pulled her smock over her head and placed it on the back of the chair. She turned off the switch controlling the air exhaust unit that she had positioned over her work to remove solvent vapours. She felt immediate relief when the noise subsided: she hadn't been conscious of the constant hum until it stopped.

In the new quiet, she also became conscious of her exhaustion. Every bone in her body was aching. She flopped over to touch her toes, stretching her back. Her muscles were just beginning to loosen when a cat tail in the face reminded her that she was expected in the kitchen.

Chapter 13

JERRY WORKED ALL WEEKEND, SLOWLY and painstakingly removing the brown paint to reveal a rich display of colour. By Monday morning there was still not a lot to see, but what there was looked exciting: strong shades of yellow competing with deep earth tones in the shadows. Breaking only for lunch and dinner, she stopped working around nine in the evening. Carol phoned shortly after, eager to know how she was getting along.

"It's amazing," she replied into the phone, her voice a mixture of fatigue and excitement.

"What do you mean?"

"The brushwork is ... you really have to see for yourself, Carol. I'm speechless. What I can see so far, is ..." Jerry broke off, unable to find the right words.

"Okay, I'm coming over tomorrow morning. I can't stand it. Is it really that good?"

"Yes, really."

Carol squeezed in the visit on her way to work. Jerry had cleaned off enough for one complete figure to be visible.

"Oh my, oh yes ... I see what you mean ..." She stood, engrossed, in front of the painting, her expression serious.

"It's incredible, isn't it?" breathed Jerry, standing by her side.

They found themselves whispering as they stood there. The glimpse of the painting exposed so far was the work of a master. The quality of the colour and brushwork was beyond anything either of them had ever seen outside a gallery. A network of hairline cracks covered the surface, and there was still some residue from the overpaint, but the quality shone through.

"I know it's too early to say," ventured Carol, "but you know who it reminds me of ..."

"Yes," Jerry broke in quickly, hoping to cut Carol off. She didn't want to hear it, she wasn't ready. Carol continued, her eyes fixed on the painting. She spoke so softly Jerry almost thought she imagined the word, but then it was what she had hardly dared to think herself.

"... Vermeer," finished Carol.

"Oh, Carol," said Jerry, as though she had said something she shouldn't have.

"It's the highlights, isn't it? No one else does them like that. But it's not exactly like him, because the rendering is more uncertain."

"Uncertain because he hasn't mastered the technique yet," replied Jerry. "It looks as though he's still finding his way — before his style was fully developed."

"An *early* Vermeer?" asked Carol her eyes wide. "Are we both mad?"

"Probably," answered Jerry abruptly, wanting to change the mood. "Let's have some tea or something. This is really getting to me."

They were naturally disturbed by their immediate impressions. After all, Vermeer was probably one of the more famous painters in the world. Little was known about him, apart from the fact that he lived from 1632 to 1675. Very few of his paintings existed, under forty altogether. Because his paintings were both famous and rare, there had been many attempts to fake his work. The best forger was a Dutch artist, van Meegeren, who was caught in the 1940s. The thing about forgeries was that they tended to carry the style of the time in which they were done. Although van Meegeren's forgeries of Vermeer were accepted in his own day, to modern eyes, some seventy years later, they appeared obvious. Now the unmistakable look of the 1940s overrode any sense that van Meegeren's Vermeers belonged to the seventeenth century.

What Jerry and Carol could see so far did not belong to the twentieth century, nor to the nineteenth. But it was much too early to tell, much more of the painting would have to be revealed before they could be certain. They sat in the kitchen and tried to find some other subject of conversation.

"Have you heard from Nick lately?" prompted Carol.

Jerry was feeling quite shy about her involvement with him. Now that they were so close, she no longer felt like sharing him, even with Carol. She admitted only that they were in daily contact by email. Jerry felt awkward. She had made it clear that she didn't want to discuss the painting, and now she had even closed up about Nick.

Carol sensed it was time to go; anyway, she would be late for work. God, Jerry could get prickly, Carol thought to herself. As much as she loved her, keeping up with her odd reactions to things was sometimes a strain. Carol prided herself on being much more straightforward.

After she had left, Jerry remained sitting at the table, still nursing her cup of tea. She felt bad about disappointing Carol and cutting her off like that. But she really did feel jumpy about the painting, and she certainly wasn't ready to talk about Nick. She stood up and rinsed out her cup in the kitchen sink. Carol's personality could be too strong for her sometimes, and this was definitely one of those times.

Jerry soon settled back into her routine of curling cotton wool around the thin stick of wood, dipping it into solvent, and rolling it across the picture. Gradually, more and more of the painting below became visible.

She continued, working intensely for several more days. Andrew phoned frequently, anxious to know how she was doing. Jerry was reluctant to tell him what she was finding. It was so momentous, she hardly wanted to admit it to herself. Finally, near the end of the week he insisted on making a visit. By then, she was so immersed in the image, she felt she had lost all objectivity. She no longer felt sure of anything, let alone Vermeer.

As usual when Andrew arrived, both cats silently vanished. He was so intent on seeing the painting that he barely nodded in her direction, heading straight for the studio. All three figures were now visible in the centre of the composition. The remains of the nineteenth-century landscape were still evident around the edges and obscured the setting in which the figures stood, but judging from the x-rays they were grouped around some rocks with trees in the background.

"Well, well," he said quietly after a few moments. "*Diana and Her Companions*. But we're missing two. Have you seen Vermeer's painting of this subject at Mauritshuis Gallery?" Jerry shook her head. She had never been to The Hague.

"I can barely believe my eyes," he said slowly. "It's very similar to the composition ... but, you know, I don't think it's a copy of that painting. Do you have a book on Vermeer? I want to check the *Diana*."

"No, sorry Andrew." Jerry had been actively avoiding looking at Vermeer's work. She had not wanted to get involved in speculation. There were so many other possibilities. After all, through the whole of history, artists had learned to paint by making copies. Even when they were well established, they still paid homage to old masters by copying their work. It was a way to understand how a particular painting was achieved. As far as she could tell, the world must be knee-deep in copies by now. And some were very good. In fact, some artists copied their own work. If the image was particularly successful and popular, they would churn out a few more, or have studio assistants do it. The idea of an artist labouring away on a single, unique, never-to-be-repeated work of art was a figment of some ancient art historian's imagination. How this idea ever took hold was beyond her. Finding a painting that looked incredibly like a Vermeer, did not mean it *was* a Vermeer. People just didn't go around finding new authentic Vermeers, she reminded herself sternly, as she had been doing for several days.

Andrew excused himself, saying he was going to fetch his book and would return shortly. She saw him out, then went back to work on the painting. He returned in less than half an hour, this time a bit breathless with excitement.

"Right, look at this Jerry," he said, pointing to a colour photograph of the painting in the Mauritshuis collection. It was a landscape with figures, very similar to what she had on her easel. "You see? It's almost the same, but the two figures in the background aren't present in our scene, and we don't have a view of the sky."

She studied the photograph. The sky appeared in the top right corner, opening the composition out, so that the figures were set in the foreground against a background of forest. In the painting on her easel, there was no sky visible at all, giving the scene a closed intimacy. With the trees no longer functioning as backdrop, but surrounding the figures, they appeared to be deep within the forest giving an entirely different feeling to the image. She also noticed that the brushwork in the Mauritshuis painting was more crudely handled. Their painting was confident, the brushstrokes that defined the drapery on the figures were easier to follow. The painting in Jerry's studio was far more developed; more sure.

"You know, Andrew, our painting looks as though it was painted after this one," she said, studying the image in the book. "Are they sure the Mauritshuis painting is by Vermeer? It's not nearly to the same standard as his other work."

"Actually, there was some debate about this piece and another one thought to be from around the same time. But now they are sure. They're considered 'juvenilia,' painted at the beginning of his career, when he was in his early twenties."

Jerry frowned with concentration, trying to remember her art history courses. "Wasn't there a composition by another painter that the *Diana* was modelled after? I seem to remember something ..."

Andrew looked back at his book, reading through the section on the *Diana*. "Yes, you're right. There was a *Diana and Her Companions* painted in 1648 by an Amsterdam painter, Jacob van Loo. It was believed by some to be the painting Vermeer based his *Diana* on." He shut the book decisively. "Well, whatever. The painting we have here is certainly not by van Loo. And it's vastly superior to the *Diana* attributed to Vermeer in this book. That's for sure.

"I think you're right, Jerry. Our painting was done after the Mauritshuis *Diana*. These changes also seem to rule out the possibility that ours is a copy; a copy would be faithful to the composition. Without the sky, and with two less figures, ours is significantly different, enough to suggest, to me at least, that it was a further working of the composition by the same artist. It's pretty hard to ignore the mastery of the forms and brushwork. Vermeer was much further along in his development when he made this painting, don't you agree?"

Jerry nodded her head, but privately she was refusing to consider the implications. If this really was a long-lost painting by Vermeer, then it was worth millions. Millions and millions and millions, repeated Jerry rather morosely to herself. It would be dreadful, she would be caught in a circus of media hype. Of course it was thrilling to be so close to this wonderful work of art. But the weight of the find was overwhelming her. She hated it.

"Hate it?!" demanded Carol when she dropped by after work and found Jerry cleaning and cursing under her breath. Andrew had gone and the cats were back in their usual places. Carol was incredulous. "What a bizarre reaction. I can't figure you out. You should be over the moon! This is a once in a lifetime find!"

"I don't trust it. It's too ... too ... I don't know. It's just too bloody unlikely. Nobody finds a Vermeer."

"I beg to differ. I think you just have," said Carol firmly.

Chapter 14

IN THE WEEK THAT FOLLOWED, JERRY FINISHED the overpaint removal and cleaned off the remaining residue covering the painting. After removing the varnish, she carefully filled in the small areas of missing paint with a mixture of chalk and synthetic glue. Her studio lights sat at a low angle to highlight the texture of the paint. Working with dentist's tools, she carved into the hardened chalk to match the surface of the surrounding paint. Using a thinned-down mixture of the fill material, she painted brushstrokes to mimic the ones on the painting. Thus a ridge of original paint, which abruptly ended where the paint was missing, was completed in chalk. Jerry loved this part of her work. It was like sculpture in miniature. This was where her professionalism really shone. When colour was applied to match the original paint, her fills would disappear, blending invisibly into the surrounding paint.

Restorers who were not professionally trained and who worked in framers' or dealers' backrooms, the sweatshops of the restoration industry, rarely had the time or inclination to go this far. The worst of them would hastily stuff putty from a hardware store into the missing spots, then heedless of the surrounding paint, quickly sand down their fills (sometimes sanding the original paint as well). No matter how well they managed to match the colour later, their fills were always visible, leaving the painting spotted with smooth glossy patches that disrupted the image and devalued its integrity.

There were very few paint losses and they were small, so it did not take long for her to complete this part of the work. Next, she brushed a very thin coat of fresh varnish over the painting to restore an even gloss and saturate the colours. Tidy spots of white from the fills now dotted the surface, waiting to be coloured in. Jerry used specially prepared paint for this. If she just went ahead and matched the colours with oil paint, in a short while the oil would darken, shifting the colours away from their original hue. Over the years the two paints would diverge even more, until the inpainting stood out as blotches of ill-matched colour. Jerry had seen examples of this on even the most famous paintings. Aside from disfiguring the image, old oil inpaints were difficult to remove without damaging the original paint.

Instead of mixing her colours in oil, she used a synthetic resin that was chemically stable. It would not change its colour as it aged, so the pigments embedded in the plastic would always match the original. The painting required very little colour matching as there were so few damages. In the end it took only two days to finish the inpainting. Then she was ready to apply the final varnish.

She had been in regular contact with Nick by email about her progress with the painting at each stage of the unveiling. It was customary to consult with a more experienced restorer when taking on a complex treatment, and she wished he were available to see the piece. Instead, she sent him scanned photographs. He was as cautious as she was about the attribution to Vermeer, but he couldn't ignore the quality of the painting either.

Jerry applied the final varnish with a spray gun. If she had tried to brush it on she would run the risk of the solvent in the varnish dissolving her inpainting and smearing the colours over the picture. The spray application allowed her to build up a series of very thin layers. She was working with a natural resin and wanted to apply it as sparingly and evenly as possible. This way, as the thin layer of resin gradually yellowed, it would not have much influence on the overall tonality of the work. By making sure the layers were even, yellowing would also be less noticeable. Old brush-coated varnishes were often unsightly because thicker patches and drips became more and more noticeable as the varnish discoloured.

Some of her colleagues chose a synthetic plastic resin for the final varnish. Like the inpainting medium she had used, it would not yellow with time. However, Jerry felt that it was difficult with synthetic varnishes to match the clarity and subtle sheen that natural resins imparted. Still it was always a tradeoff. The natural resin would inevitably yellow. To remove it meant subjecting the paint to another round of solvents. Synthetic resins might not look as good, but in theory, they were there indefinitely and the paint need not be exposed to potentially damaging solvents again.

Her treatment of the painting had taken a little over a month. With the last coat of varnish applied, it was just a matter of waiting for it to dry, then the painting could be moved to the Toronto auction house for authentication, the first step in having it sold. Andrew told her that the owner wanted to have it ready for the "Important Old Master" sale in New York, which always took place near the end of May, now only a few weeks away. If they missed it, the next one, in London, would not be until July.

Although close, the timing would work out fine. While she waited for the solvent to evaporate from the varnish, the painting remained with Jerry. She found its presence distracting now that the restoration was completed. Although she tried to concentrate on removing the varnish from a portrait she had started earlier, she found her eyes regularly straying to the Vermeer.

"What a jewel of a painting," she said as she put down her swab and walked over to it for the third time that morning. The lead-tin yellow sparkled, now fully saturated under the fresh varnish. The density and solidity of the passages painted with this yellow surpassed anything she had seen (except, of course, for another Vermeer). The blue in the central figure's skirt was equally intense, the paint was thick and heavy with colour.

In the drapery the demarcation of planes was bold and sure, reminding her of Vermeer's *Guitar-Player*. When she was at the Chelsea, she lived close to Hampstead Heath, and often walked through the forest and parkland to visit the painting at Kenwood, the grand historic house at the edge of the heath. There was a strangely out-of-focus feeling to the image of a woman playing a guitar in the Kenwood picture. It had something to do with the way the highlights were rendered as many individual spots of thick paint. She saw the same treatment in the painting on her easel. Jerry had given up resisting the idea that this was a genuine Vermeer and allowed herself to drink in the colours and confident brushwork without reserve. "It's so beautiful ...," she sighed, knowing she would miss the thrill of having it so near.

It was curious that the owner did not want to visit Jerry's studio to see it. When she broached the subject, Andrew was impatient with her. The owner had purchased it as an investment, and he was keeping track of Jerry's progress with the photographs she had been handing over to Andrew at each stage of the work.

"Still, it seems strange that he wouldn't be eager to see it for himself," she persisted. Andrew grew very quiet. It was obvious he would not be drawn into any conversation with her about the mysterious owner.

Jerry was bracing herself for the moment when the painting would be on display at the auction house, anticipating that she might be on display along with it, especially when the press were invited in. Andrew had asked her to be there when two of the leading art experts were brought in to authenticate it. She was looking forward to meeting the Dutch art historian; she had read some of his scholarly papers. His research relied on technical information as well as historical documentation, and he appeared to have a sound grasp of the materials in use at the time Vermeer was painting. It would be very interesting to hear his opinion. Meeting the other expert, Sir Alfred Wentworth-Baltham, or Sir Wentworth-Wet-Bottom, as her friend Patricia had called him, was another matter. Jerry had been introduced to him numerous times at exhibition openings in London. He was invariably condescending and dismissive. An obnoxious man, she thought. He had published many papers as well, but they mainly consisted of great sweeping statements of opinion with little scholarly content. He was not someone she looked forward to sharing this painting with.

Chapter 15

FINALLY, THE DAY ARRIVED. Jerry stood beside Andrew in the showroom at the auction house. She spread the results of the technical study and analyses on a table near the easel where the painting now sat. Since the sides and back of the painting would be examined as well, it was unframed, and therefore looked a little vulnerable sitting alone in such opulent surroundings. There were gilt decorations and red curtains everywhere. It all seemed a little overdone, like some nineteenth-century ballroom. The fresh varnish on the painting still gave off a slight odour of resin and turpentine.

As usual, Andrew was impeccably tailored. He really is quite beautiful, she thought as she stole a glance at his profile. Too bad he's so cold. He's probably the best looking man I've ever seen, even better looking than Nick, she admitted. But Nick was so much more appealing; he was funny and lively. Andrew's polish was admirable, his manners charming, but she certainly didn't crave his company. Standing beside Andrew, Jerry was completely unaware that her own looks complemented his. She was wearing a simple sleeveless black dress. Knowing that her fine features and slight build made her appear young, she had chosen a severe tailored look. In the end, she appeared elegant and remote, just like Andrew.

They were both growing restless, waiting for the owner of the auction house to arrive. He was flying in from the head offices in London. The British and Dutch art historians were due at the same time. Staff at the Toronto branch had gathered in the hallway, the air electric with anticipation.

Early that morning, Nick had woken Jerry with exciting news. Roger, his colleague at Cambridge University, had found copal resin in the paint sample from the Vermeer that Nick had brought back from Ottawa. There was a centuries-old debate on whether or not the old masters had added resin to their oil paint. Mérimée, one of the best-known nineteenth-century authors, had surmised from the visual quality of their paint that they had used resin, and suggested that it would be a hard fossil resin like copal. In his day there had been no certain method for analyzing the medium to discover if this theory was true, therefore it had remained an academic debate.

The search for the missing medium of the old master painters had been already well underway in the eighteenth and nineteenth centuries. Painters, examining old masters' works and discovering the exceptionally luscious translucency of the paint, assumed that they were privy to some technical secret: a medium, like copal varnish, that when added to their paint would allow them such fluidity and control. Attempts in the late 1970s and early '80s to analyze the medium in old paintings had not found copal resin, so it was assumed that it had not been used.

Nick's research on artists' technical treatises and manuals from the nineteenth century had uncovered documentary evidence pointing to the use of copal at that time, but strangely, even where an artist had written notes saying he had used it in a painting, medium analysis still did not find any evidence of it. Then it was discovered that copal was invisible to the method of analysis which had been commonly in use. With new, more sensitive instrumentation, evidence of very early use of resin in oil paint was gradually building. Nick, who had always believed that the old masters had used resin, was extremely pleased with the results from the Vermeer. He wanted Jerry to write a paper with him about this discovery. He was planning to send what was left of the paint sample to a laboratory in The Netherlands where they were able to distinguish one copal resin from another.

"Wow," she had said. "I didn't know they could identify the *exact* copal resin used. That's amazing!"

"It's very recent," replied Nick. "A team of chemists studying the molecular basis of oil painting materials has worked out a method for sorting the different fossil resins in the copal group. They're eager for good samples to work with, so they were happy to take this on ..."

Jerry had to interrupt Nick at that point; she had suddenly noticed the time and realized she would be late at the auction house. Wishing her good luck he had hung up, and she rushed to get ready, forgetting all about the conversation with Nick until she was standing next to Andrew as they waited in the showroom for the others to arrive.

Beside her, Andrew gave an impatient sigh. Jerry hurried to fill the tense silence. She started to tell him about the medium analysis of the Vermeer and what Nick had found.

Andrew's body immediately stiffened and a dark scowl crossed his flawless features. He turned to look at her and said forcefully, "Listen, Jerry, I thought I had made it clear that you were *not* to go ahead with any analyses of the medium; it's too costly and it's not necessary!"

Surprised at the vehemence of his reaction, she said, "But it's not costing anything. Nick has found some researchers in Holland who are willing to do it without charging us ..."

"Shush! not now," he hissed as a group of dark-suited men entered the room. Their attention was completely taken up for the next few hours as they explained the restoration work. The art historians had already been sent copies of all the photographs of cross-sections and documentation surrounding the Vermeer and its recovery, but this was their first opportunity to see the originals and the painting itself.

Old Wet-bottom was swanning about the room, extolling the virtues of the painting in a loud voice. He barely acknowledged Jerry and her documentation. Thankfully, the Dutch art historian was perfectly charming and spent a good deal of his time poring over the analytical results and discussing them with her. Or at least he tried to. Every time he asked a question, Andrew, who was hovering at her side, would break in and take over. She was surprised at this annoying, more forceful side of his character. She didn't particularly care about being sidelined, but the Dutch art historian seemed disconcerted by Andrew's overbearing manner.

Just before noon, they were ushered into another grand room for lunch. Jerry found herself pecking at her food, wishing she could disappear back to her loft, slip into some baggy clothes, and be alone. But she was not going to get away that easily: the afternoon ground on, and hours later she was still on call for questions. When it was time for the experts to make their decision, Andrew and the auction house owner joined them, leaving Jerry in the showroom with the Vermeer. She was rarely alone as staff members from the auction house kept popping into the room, obviously unable to concentrate on their own work while they too waited.

Eventually the men emerged, relaxed and smiling. As they walked into the room Jerry caught Andrew's eye. He nodded. It was confirmed, the press would be on their way.

The next few hours with the press were gruelling. Although confident in her work and her profession, Jerry was essentially quite shy. To her embarrassment, the TV cameras and reporters turned their attention to her, delighted with the dramatic story of her discovery of one painting hidden beneath another. Andrew seemed put out that she stole the limelight and so was Old Wetbottom, she noticed with some pleasure. Finally the TV crews and reporters packed up their equipment and Jerry could go.

Home at last, she kicked off her shoes and sank gratefully onto the couch. Alvin and Tony grabbed the opportunity to purr their welcome and managed to transfer the better part of both their coats onto her black dress in a flurry of affection.

"Come on, you guys, get off me!" she protested, laughing, as she pushed ineffectually at the swarming cats. "You would think I hadn't been home for a week!" She got up to feed them and take a few pills for the headache that had been dogging her all day. After changing into her favourite nightgown with her terry-towel bathrobe wrapped around her, she curled up on the couch and dialled Nick.

"It's been declared authentic! They said it really is a Vermeer, isn't that incredible!?"

"Jerry, that's great. Wonderful news. You must be so pleased. I know you were worried about the press. How did that go?"

"Not quite as bad as I thought. The unexpected bit was Andrew. He was a real pain," she continued, describing Andrew's objection to the medium analysis, and his pushy behaviour when she was trying to speak to the Dutch art historian.

Jerry ended up on the phone for most of the evening. After a chat with Nick, she called Carol and gave her a full account of the day. Then she switched on the TV, carefully avoiding the news. Carol said she'd tape it for her, she didn't want to face herself in the media just yet. Around eleven, she began to feel sleepy, the tension of the day finally behind her. She followed her normal routine, fed Alvin and Tony their bedtime treats, and climbed gratefully into bed. At around midnight, after reading herself into a stupor, she switched off the light.

In what seemed like only moments later, Jerry was wide awake. What had awoken her? Her alarm clock said it was 2:30 a.m. She was just settling back onto her pillows when she heard a noise and froze, straining to listen. The sound was unmistakable. It was the slow turning of a key ... the key to her front door.

Out of bed in seconds, she stood in the dark room, her heart pounding, adrenalin pumping. "What can I do ... what can I do ...," she whispered frantically to herself. She felt a soft brush against her legs and looked down to see a blur of Alvin and Tony heading for their spot behind the laundry basket.

"Another break-in ... Shit! Maybe if they think I'm asleep they'll take what they want and leave ...," she thought wildly. It seemed crazy, but she started shoving pillows under the duvet into a body shape. Then she silently ran for the bedroom closet.

She got there just in time. Peering through a crack in the louvered doors she could see her bedroom door, which was slightly ajar. It slowly swung open. All she could make out was a shadowy shape and a hand encased in black resting on the door handle. Whoever it was stood there a long time. Her lungs were bursting, she had to remind herself to breathe. Her legs started to shake from the awkward half-kneeling position she was in. Just when she thought she couldn't hold still another second, the hand was gone, the shape had moved away. Thank god, she thought as she quietly repositioned herself.

She could hear movements in the studio. They must be after the paintings. It's probably the same people who were here before, but how the hell did they get a key? So much for the new chains on the door, she thought disgustedly. The locksmith warned her they could be cut, too, but she hadn't quite believed him, they looked so strong. She listened intently, she had been assuming there were two people, but it was hard to tell, there could be only one. Anyway, there was nothing for them to find. She had completed her last piece the day before and the storage shelves were empty.

"Just go, just go ...," she repeated over and over, willing whoever it was to leave without coming back to the bedroom. Sounds in the kitchen: what was going on in there? Then the front door opened and closed. The key again.

"They're locking the door after themselves? What the hell kind of thieves lock the door behind them?" she whispered.

Shifting her position slightly, Jerry waited in the closet, wanting to be sure they were gone, still too scared to venture out. Then she smelled it.

"Gas? ... Is that gas?!" She scrambled out of the closet and flew to the bedroom door. There the smell was even stronger and she could hear it hissing out of her stove. She started towards the kitchen with the intention of turning it off. She was half-way there when she caught sight of the light on in her microwave. As she drew nearer, she could see something revolving around inside and could hear the low characteristic hum of the fan and the motor. Whatever was inside was metal, there were small sparks on the surface. It was some kind of metal cylinder, a canister ... an aerosol canister!

"It's going to blow any second!" There was no time to think. She twisted around abruptly and started running towards the bedroom. She pushed up the window sash as far as it would go. Her only thought was to get out onto the fire escape as fast as possible. She shoved the laundry basket away from the wall with her foot, leaned down and grabbed a cat in each arm. Tony immediately started to squirm. As she dropped Alvin onto the fire escape platform outside the window, she lost her grip on Tony who jumped back inside the apartment. "Tony, stop!!" she ordered. The sheer panic in her voice made him flatten and freeze in mid-flight. She swooped down and grabbed him again. As she turned back towards the window, she saw her purse on her wicker chair and managed to catch it up with one hand just before climbing through.

The metal stairs on the fire escape were numbingly cold and

rough on her bare feet. Thankfully it was only three flights to the street. By the time she was on the grass at the bottom, Alvin was nowhere to be seen, but she was still holding Tony tightly in her arms. The night air was frigid, the grass soggy with spring. She crossed the lawn, then felt every stone on the sidewalk as she rushed to her car. She was trying to get her keys out of her handbag while holding on to Tony at the same time. It was an impossible juggling act and Tony won. He hit the ground at a run.

Jerry got the car door open and collapsed into her seat, shaking uncontrollably from cold and fear. She started the engine, desperate to get away as fast as she could. She gripped the steering wheel and started to put the car in gear. Then she stopped. She knew she couldn't just leave the cats. Cursing, she got out of the car and stood calling them. Of course, they had vanished. How the hell could she find them now? It was crazy to be risking her life for two cats. Then she knew what to do.

Frantically, she raced around to the passenger side, opened the door and whistled. They materialized out of nowhere and jumped into the car, just as they did at the end of every walk. She scrambled back in and threw the car into gear. They were about half a block away when she heard the explosion. She fixed her eyes on the road ahead and kept driving.

※

Carol's apartment building had an underground parking lot. She had given the entry code to Jerry, so it was easy for her to drive straight in. She would not have to walk any farther than necessary in her bare feet with two struggling cats. From the car she dialled Carol's number on her cellphone. "Pick up, pick up ... pick up ...," she chanted to herself as the phone rang. Moments later, a groggy voice answered.

Jerry sat at Carol's kitchen table, wrapped in one of her bathrobes, a pair of heavy woollen socks on her feet. It barely registered that the glass of wine she had just downed was having absolutely no effect. Her hands were still shaking. Was it being chilled or being frightened, or both? They seemed to be the only part of her reacting normally — the rest simply felt numb. She had just lost every single possession. She couldn't believe it.

"I guess I'd better call the police and tell them what happened," she said to Carol, not wanting to move.

"What do you think *did* happen? Why would art thieves turn on your gas and set up your microwave to explode?"

Jerry was having trouble thinking clearly. She didn't answer.

"Listen, Jerry," Carol said, leaning towards her from across the table and speaking slowly, "it doesn't make sense; art thieves want something to fence. They don't go around trying to kill people."

"I guess I should phone the police," she repeated stupidly, not taking in anything Carol had said.

"We have to think this through first," continued Carol. "These guys have a key to your loft. They let themselves in, check that you're sleeping like a baby, turn on the gas, put an aerosol can in the microwave, then leave and lock the door behind them. Your loft goes up in an explosion ..."

"It sounded huge," interrupted Jerry.

"Okay, a huge explosion. By the way, why didn't you just shut off the microwave and the gas?"

Jerry rolled her eyes, it was just like Carol to challenge her at a moment like this. "Carol, I panicked!" A slight edge of hysteria crept into her voice. "All I wanted to do was to get out of there!"

"Okay, Okay. Maybe it was for the best," she said soothingly. "It might've been more dangerous to try anything at that point anyway, who knows, the slightest spark could've set the gas off." Carol sat back in her chair. "The thing is, they probably think you're dead. If you call the police, your would-be killer or killers might find out you're still alive, right? Then they would want to kill you all over again. I think we'd better sleep on this tonight, and decide about calling the police tomorrow. It could be to your advantage to stay dead for a while."

Carol made up the sofa bed. Jerry crawled in with a nagging feeling that she should be calling the police. But she had no energy to argue, all she wanted to do was sleep. Maybe this was some extended nightmare that would be gone in the morning. She called softly to the cats. They jumped up and picked their way over the covers to her, snuggling as close as they could. She stroked them, told them how wonderful they were, and somewhere in the middle of a sentence, she fell fast asleep.

Carol's voice came to Jerry as if from far away. She tried to roll over, to go deeper into sleep, but despite her efforts she came swimming to the surface. Carol was standing over her, shaking her shoulder, "Jerry, Jerry ... wake up, Jerry," Carol was repeating.

"What?" she answered thickly.

"I just thought about your car. We have to take it back to your loft. If your car is gone, they'll know you survived."

"Oh, god," she groaned, "I can't move, I'm so tired. Can't we just leave it here? No one will see it in your garage," she pleaded.

"No, it has to be near the loft. Come on Jerry, they could go back anytime and notice it's gone. I need you to drive. We'll take both cars and come back in mine. Here, I have some clothes for you. You can wear my running shoes, they'll probably fit."

Jerry found herself dragging on clothes, her body protesting. Her skin was hypersensitive and achy, the fabric felt rough and strange. She was light-headed and she had trouble getting her hands to tie the laces on Carol's shoes. Meanwhile Carol, all purpose and energy, was bustling around the apartment finding car keys and getting an extra sweater for Jerry.

They arrived on Jerry's street to find it alight with flashing fire engines and emergency vehicles. A multitude of water hoses snaked across the road making it impossible to get very close by car. Jerry found a parking space and pulled into it quickly. It was a good half-block away from her loft, but surely no one would question that. Carol drew up beside her. Jerry locked her car and got inside with Carol.

"I'm going to drive a little closer and leave you in the car for a moment while I go and ask the firefighter what happened."

"No, please, Carol, can't we just go home now? We *know* what happened." Jerry thought she had crossed the line from sounding plaintive to outright whining. She longed for sleep; it seemed to be some kind of reaction to the shock. She could barely keep her eyes open. By now it must be four in the morning.

But Carol was determined. She left Jerry sagging in the car seat and marched off towards the building, still ablaze. A few minutes later Jerry heard another car moving slowly past. She glanced over and thought she saw Andrew driving. Instinctively she ducked out of sight. She had already been slumped down in her seat, trying to pretend to her body that she was in bed. It was still very dark, so she was sure he had not seen her. "What the hell is he doing? He doesn't live around here," she thought angrily to herself, then reconsidered. "That can't be right. It probably wasn't him; it could've been anybody. I'm too tired to even see straight." She wriggled in a huff and settled even deeper into the seat, staring straight ahead, trying very hard to think of nothing.

When Carol came back, she filled Jerry in on what she had found out. "They know it was a gas explosion. They don't seem to suspect foul play. They're worried because they know there was someone living in the loft, but they haven't been able to get inside. There's still a hell of a fire and that has them puzzled. It's much hotter and more advanced than it should be for a gas explosion."

"The solvents," said Jerry quietly. Her solvent cupboard was fireproof only to a certain temperature and certainly not explosion proof. Once they started to burn, the temperature would go very high indeed.

"Good news," Carol continued. "A reporter was there, taking it all down while I was chatting with the firefighter. It should be in the papers in the morning."

"Famous Vermeer restorer killed in studio fire?" asked Jerry, trying out the headlines.

"Hopefully, something like that. You'd better phone Nick before he hears about it."

Chapter 16

SATURDAY MORNING, DETECTIVE-SERGEANT WIENS from the art fraud unit sat with Jerry in Carol's living room while Carol made coffee. Jerry, looking pale and tired, was finding his endless questions impossible.

"So you don't know anyone who would want to blow up your apartment with you in it?" he persisted.

Carol came back into the room with a tray of steaming coffee and warm croissants. "We've been over that about a million times, Officer. Neither of us can think why this would happen," she interjected. "Jerry just uncovered an incredibly valuable painting by one of the world's most famous artists, but it's at the auction house. There was so much publicity yesterday, no art thief could possibly have thought she still had it. And anyway, why try to kill her?"

"It has to be related to the Vermeer," he said, helping himself to a croissant. "Was there anything unusual about the painting?"

"No," Jerry responded, her voice small. The shock of the night before was still with her. "That is, not really ...," she continued, thinking aloud, "except for the resin in the paint. But Nick thinks it's probably not unusual; it's just that we haven't been able to detect resin very well with our methods of analysis until fairly recently ...," she trailed off.

Carol could see Jerry was not up to lengthy explanations, so she filled Detective-Sergeant Wiens in on the search for the secret of the old masters' medium and how Nick had called to say they'd found resin in the paint used in the Vermeer.

"Did you tell anyone about what Nick found?" he asked Jerry more gently.

"Just Carol," she answered, then she frowned, "and Andrew

of course. I told him yesterday, while we were waiting at the auction house. He wasn't very happy about it. He seemed to resent us continuing with analysis." She picked up her coffee cup, and continued with mild irritation, "The Vermeer is *fine*, the presence of resin is really only of interest to a small academic group ..."

"Well," he said, sitting back in his chair and brushing croissant flakes off his lap, "I agree with Carol. I think it's in your best interest right now not to surface for a while. As a matter of fact ..." Wiens was interrupted by his cellphone. As he listened his eyebrows shot up in surprise and he looked over at Jerry. "Thank you," he said putting the phone down. "They've found evidence of human remains in the debris from your loft," he announced gravely, then paused, looking suspiciously at Jerry. "You said no one else lived in the building?"

"Oh, my god!" said Jerry. "No, no one lives there but me. The rest of the building is used as a warehouse." She sat still, trying to absorb what he had said. Someone was killed in her studio? How could that be?

"Was it a man or a woman, do they know?" asked Carol.

"They don't know yet. All that's left are ash and bone fragments."

There was a shocked silence. Then Jerry met Carol's gaze.

"Alice!!" both women cried at once. They began to laugh, their relief mixed with an edge of hysteria.

Wiens eyed them dubiously. "*Who* is Alice?"

Jerry explained: Alice was the anatomical skeleton she kept in her studio.

"But surely they'll be able to tell that — the bones were held together with wires. There must be holes and at least some evidence of the wires left?" she asked.

"Yes, when the bones are investigated more closely, that will no doubt become apparent." He took out his phone. "But this could work to our advantage." Wiens explained the nature of the remains to his colleagues. "Contact the press and tell them that human remains have been found. Nothing more. Is that clear?"

Having decided on a course of action, the phlegmatic Detective-Sergeant now became quite efficient. "Is there anywhere you can go where you won't be recognized — preferably out of the country?" he asked.

"I can probably arrange something through Nick," she answered.

"Good," he replied, then he turned to Carol. "What about you? Can we reach you here for the next week or so?"

"No," replied Carol. "I was planning to go up north to open up my cottage for the season."

"Is there a telephone?"

"No, it's pretty remote."

"What about your cellphone?" Jerry interjected.

"Doesn't work up there. I guess there are not enough people around to make it worthwhile for them to have services in that area," responded Carol.

"Well, we should know how to find you," said Wiens.

"That's easy," replied Carol going to a little desk where her telephone sat in the front hallway of her apartment. She rummaged around in the top drawer. "Ah, here. I thought I might still have some of these," she said pleased with her find. As she handed him a hand-drawn map, she explained, "It's a map we made for guests years ago when my parents were still alive. The directions are quite clear."

Jerry called Nick from Carol's bedroom for the second time that day. They had been on the phone earlier when she had called to tell him about the explosion. She reached him easily at his flat in Cambridge.

"Could you come here?" he asked, when she explained the Detective-Sergeant's suggestion.

"Someone might recognize me."

"Wait a minute, I have an idea. One of my friends has a holiday home on the Continent. It's in a tiny out-of-the-way spot. Let me call him and see if it's free; then we can stay there."

"We?"

"You don't think I'm going to leave you on your own, do you?" he said brusquely. "I have some holidays coming to me, and this seems to be a perfect time to use them. I'll ring you back as soon as possible."

Monday evening, Jerry was on a plane heading to Nice. She had left Carol with the odious task of phoning Jerry's colleagues and friends, pretending that she thought her best friend was dead. Carol had had to arrange a lot of things, including having Jerry's car towed to her underground parking, a bit of theatre Detective-Sergeant Wiens recommended to ensure that Jerry's death appeared convincing. Of course Jerry still had her keys, but Wiens thought it might look suspicious if Carol just showed up and drove away with the car. Jerry's death would not be formalized until there had been a positive identification of the human remains found in her loft. In the meantime, everyone would assume the bones were hers. Wiens didn't know how long she would have to remain in hiding; he wanted her out of sight until after the Vermeer was sold. It was being auctioned in New York that week during the "Important Old Masters" sale.

The Sergeant-Detective suggested that Jerry be driven down to Buffalo where she could fly to La Guardia before boarding the plane to Nice. That way she would avoid being recognized in the Toronto airport.

"Is that really necessary?" she asked doubtfully. "Surely the chances of my running into someone I know in the airport are very remote?"

He reminded her that her face and name had just been all over the papers and TV because of her find of the Vermeer. For the moment she was a bit of a media personality. They shouldn't take any chances. Jerry agreed meekly; she had completely forgotten about her short burst of fame.

She organized her flight, paying for it with Carol's credit card since hers could not be active while she was "dead," and marvelled at how easy it was to make all the necessary arrangements without leaving the apartment. She would eventually get insurance money from the loft. She had been well insured, enough to pay back the loans for her studio equipment and then some. But for now, her affairs had to be suspended and it seemed that she had no other choice but to disappear.

The evening before she left, Alvin and Tony had been restless. They prowled around Carol's apartment sniffing and meowing, sensing something was up. They were so preoccupied they forgot their habitual animosity. That night, as they arranged themselves on the bed to be as close as possible to Jerry, their tails almost touched.

Chapter 17

TUESDAY MORNING, NICK WAS WAITING FOR HER in the cool, white arrivals hall in Nice. She looked smaller than when he had seen her last, as though shrunken by her ordeal. He gathered her in his arms, holding her tightly. Jerry was exhausted and relieved to see him. All she wanted to do was collapse.

As she and Nick approached the rental car, he got out a map and the directions his friend had sent and asked her to take them, along with a set of car keys.

"You don't expect me to drive, do you?" she asked, alarmed at the prospect of plunging straight into city traffic.

"No, not at all," he reassured her quickly. "I got an extra set in case we lose mine or lock them in. I just want you to hold on to them." He stopped and studied her, noting the dark circles under her eyes and the pale skin. "Do you feel up to being the navigator?" he asked gently.

"Yes, of course." Some of her fatigue fell away as she looked around her. Even the airport parking lot had beds of flowers, green grass, and lush vegetation. "The air is so warm; this is lovely. May in Toronto has been freezing. It's done nothing but rain." She started to perk up with the sunshine and heavy scent of flowers in the air. It was good to be with Nick again, and to be so far from her troubles. She felt the worry that had been with her since the night of the explosion begin to evaporate in the reassuring heat.

"Is the flat nearby?" she asked as she got into the large silver-grey Citroën that Nick had arranged for them.

"It's not in France; it's just over the border in Italy, about an hour's drive from here."

"Italy! I love the idea of being in Italy, what a treat," she said enthusiastically. "But I used all the cash Carol lent me to buy French francs."

"Don't worry, they take both in most of the towns along the border. It won't be a problem. Anyway, I have plenty."

They followed the directions easily, taking the autoroute out of Nice and across the border into Italy. Sitting beside him in the car, Jerry felt protected and secure in his presence, which she was guiltily enjoying.

Soon they were in Ventimile, or Ventimiglia, as it was called in Italian. There they got thoroughly lost. The city was crammed with traffic. The directions no longer made sense, and they were bogged down in some busy dusty street. Nick rolled down his window and asked the way from a passerby, who stood inches from the car — the streets were narrow as well as congested. With a lot of hand gestures, smiles and nods, Nick gleaned enough to get them to the next major intersection. There Jerry caught sight of a sign. "Look Nick, to the left, Dolceacqua! That's what we want, isn't it?"

Out of Ventimiglia, they followed a small road that wound its way up the valley away from the sea between tall, grassy hills. Trees, perched along the crest of the hills, followed their gentle outline. The road wound on and on, carrying them up into the hills. Jerry was just beginning to wonder if it went anywhere at all, when they rounded a bend, and in front of them lay the picturesque medieval hill town of Dolceacqua, its castle perched high on top of a hill. As they passed by, Nick pointed to a beautiful stone bridge that stretched in a graceful arch over the river separating the old town from the new.

"That's the bridge Monet painted. He made Dolceacqua famous. It certainly is beautiful, isn't it?"

Jerry murmured something in assent; she was overwhelmed by the lovely scene in front of her. If only she could pretend they were on vacation, it would be perfect.

They continued up the valley to another hill town, much smaller and less impressive than Dolceacqua. Nick pulled into a parking lot. As Jerry got out of the car, feeling the air which was much cooler than in Nice, she was surprised at how cramped she felt. Her legs were aching, and the fatigue came back in a wave.

"It's not far now; it should be just a short walk," Nick reassured her.

He grabbed his bag from the trunk, and they started up the narrow passageway leading into the centre of the town. He was reading the directions; with a few rights then lefts, then over a small bridge, they soon found themselves in front of a highly polished door. As he opened it, Nick said, "Tom just finished renovating. This is my first visit. He's been working on it for a couple of years, whenever he's had some holidays."

"What made him decide to come to this place?"

"The hill towns around here are the newest frontier for renovators. Closer to Nice, the untouched places have all been bought up and now the prices are too high. In this area, there are still plenty of homes owned by old people who want something modern and more manageable. Their children have moved away to the big cities and don't want to come back to the family home. Some of the houses have stood empty for years. Tom found this one going dirt cheap. The last time it was modernized was in the twenties."

"So was this an investment for Tom? Will he sell it?"

"That's what he's hoping. He's already got his eye on another house up the street."

They peered into an inky black entrance. Nick read Tom's instructions; they needed to climb the stairs in order to find the main switch for the electricity. Jerry rummaged around in her handbag, and produced a small flashlight.

"You seem to have everything you need in there," laughed Nick.

"Well, as it happens, it's also everything I *have*," she replied; her handbag being the only thing left of her worldly possessions aside from her car.

The flat was small, but beautifully renovated. The walls were a soft smooth plaster with a subtle mottled finish. There was a sitting room immediately past the stairs from the street; then more stairs to the next floor which had a nice-sized bedroom and a lovely modern bathroom with a bathtub, which Jerry longed to soak in. Up another set of stairs was the kitchen, tiny but well designed. Sliding glass doors led out onto a terrace, looking out onto a sunny view of the hill town's clay roofs and small balconies.

Nick ran a hot bath for Jerry. She climbed in gratefully and almost dozed off. After a bit, Nick came in with an oversized bath towel and one of his T-shirts for her to wear. Climbing into bed, she was asleep the moment her head hit the pillow. Late in the afternoon, he came into the bedroom with a steaming cup of tea, and gently woke her. She felt thick and groggy, but forced herself to sit up. Nick sat on the bed beside her chatting while she sipped her tea.

She smiled at him, feeling her old self again. "Why don't you join me? It's very comfortable in this bed."

"I thought you'd never ask," he grinned.

It seemed like such a long time since they had been together in Ottawa that weekend in March. So much had happened in between. Jerry felt she knew Nick well through their daily emails. But their written intimacy had not translated immediately to being face to face. She felt more shy with him now than she had when they first met. How odd to be feeling so separate after sharing so much in writing.

At first she found it awkward to be with him, but after they had made love, she was completely reassured. The ease and naturalness of being together was back. She rolled over and ran her hand along his back; she kissed his shoulder, feeling the warmth of his skin. Toronto seemed a million miles away.

The next morning, Nick woke before Jerry and dressed quietly, trying not to disturb her. He headed out to find them some breakfast. As he stepped out onto the narrow cobblestoned street, he could smell the sweet mixture of hot pastry and freshly roasted coffee. He had only to follow his nose, and after several twists and turns down increasingly narrow passageways, he found the source: a small coffee-bar. By the time he was back, Jerry was up. They sat outside on the terrace on benches at Tom's makeshift picnic table, enjoying their coffee and brioche. The view across the rooftops took in the low hills surrounding the town. The air was mild, the sun a deep warm and rich yellow. Jerry was still wearing Nick's T-shirt; her wardrobe consisted only of a pair of black slacks and a long baggy sweater borrowed from Carol. Her hair was tangled from sleep and she looked pale and drawn. Nick eyed her with concern. The attempt on her life immediately following the excitement over the Vermeer had taken its toll.

"Jerry, lets go over what happened again. I agree with Detective-Sergeant Wiens that it has to be related to the Vermeer, but like you, I don't see how yet," he said, taking a sip of coffee.

"Okay, where shall we start ...," she replied. She mulled it over. "What about the explosion? Someone wanted me dead, presumably to stop me from revealing something, let's say about the Vermeer. But what? So far there hasn't been anything suspicious about the painting."

"You told me that Andrew was upset when you mentioned we found resin in the paint. Why would he care?"

"I thought it was the additional expense for the analysis. That seemed to be what he was worried about. I was trying to tell him it wouldn't cost anything when we were interrupted by the others coming in."

"But that doesn't make sense. The Vermeer will bring him and the owner millions. They couldn't possibly be fussing over a few thousand dollars at this point."

Jerry frowned. "Well, he sure didn't like the idea of any further investigation into the paint ..."

"Oh, that reminds me!" interrupted Nick. "I forgot all about sending the sample to The Netherlands last week." He looked down at his watch. "Oscar should be at work by now. I'll ring him right away. Perhaps he has some news for us about the copal resin in the paint."

While Nick was in the kitchen phoning his colleague in Amsterdam, she sat gazing at the view, feeling the hot sun digging through Nick's black T-shirt into the skin across her shoulders. The warmth was so comforting, the sky a beautiful cloudless blue. She was just thinking of going inside for more coffee when Nick reappeared on the terrace.

He stood looking at her with an odd expression on his face. She cupped her hand over her eyes to cut the glare of the sun as she looked back at him.

"What is it?" she asked cautiously.

He remained where he was standing. "I talked to Oscar. There was a break-in at the lab last night, and the paint sample from the Vermeer is missing."

"What! That's incredible!" she cried. "But that means we won't know about the resin now."

"No, we do know about the resin. Oscar ran the sample yesterday afternoon, before the break-in. They only got what was left over."

"Did he say? Does he know what it is?" she asked eagerly.

Nick came over and sat beside her on the bench. He took her hand and said quietly, "Jerry. The copal resin Oscar identified is kauri resin."

"Is that important? What is kauri resin?" she demanded urgently.

"Kauri resin comes from New Zealand. It wasn't introduced until the early nineteenth century. Your Vermeer couldn't have been painted prior to that. It's not a genuine Vermeer after all."

"Wow," she breathed. She sat completely still, her mind reeling. Then she stiffened, her eyes wide. "Andrew must have known. That's why he didn't want us to do more analysis. He was afraid we would find out ...," she stopped. What little colour was left in her face drained away completely as it dawned on her. "Nick," she said slowly, "it must have been Andrew who ...," she stared straight ahead and cried out, "Damn! I saw him!"

"Where? When?" asked Nick.

"The night of the explosion, when Carol insisted we take my car back. I was sitting in her car waiting for her and I saw him go by. I wondered what he was doing there, he doesn't live anywhere near my street." She continued, working it out, "He was checking to see if the explosion succeeded!" She shuddered, remembering how close Andrew had been to spotting her.

Nick gave her a hug, and holding her in his arms, he said quietly, "We still haven't got anything on him yet."

She twisted out of his embrace, incredulous. "What do you mean? He tried to kill me! He must have known it was a fake, otherwise why kill me to hide the evidence?"

"Jerry, think about it. There's no proof that Andrew and the owner knew it wasn't a genuine Vermeer. All we have now is that the painting couldn't have been made before the nineteenth century. They can say they bought the painting in good faith as a nineteenth-century copy of an earlier painting. *You* were the one who found the so-called Vermeer underneath."

She shook her head, trying to clear her thoughts. "That would explain why the painting was stolen." She rolled her eyes. "And the bloody door key. I couldn't figure out how it got off its hook and onto the kitchen counter that day Tony knocked it onto the floor. Andrew must have had it copied and left it on the counter!"

"That explains how they could get in so easily," replied Nick. "Pretty clever, they had the painting stolen *before* the Vermeer was revealed. That way they could establish, with a lot of publicity, that the painting had been completely overpainted beforehand. It would look like they couldn't have known what they had."

"They were pulling all the strings. I feel so stupid," said Jerry bitterly. "I've been set up and used all the way along."

"At least they won't get their millions," he said as he stood up and started clearing the table. "As soon as we tell your man in Toronto, they'll inform the auction house owners who will arrange their own analysis and find the same thing we have. The painting will not be sold as a genuine Vermeer, you can count on that."

"I wonder if it's still in Toronto. What is this, Wednesday? They must have flown it to New York by now. The auction is going on this week." Jerry was piling dishes from the table to help clear up when she suddenly stopped. "Nick, until this is made public, they'll be trying to eliminate anything, and anyone who could get in the way of the sale. That means you, too!"

Chapter 18

I T WAS TEN-THIRTY IN THE MORNING IN ITALY, only four-thirty a.m. in Toronto. Jerry called Detective-Sergeant Wiens's number anyway, thinking there might be someone on night duty she could speak to. There was no answer.

"Don't you have his cellphone number?" asked Nick.

"Yes. I tried that, too. He must have it switched off for the night. I left a message."

They decided they'd return Nick's rental car to the airport since it was the easiest way for him to be traced. Jerry could rent another one, along with a new cellphone. No one would be looking for her.

"It's a good thing I'm dead already," she laughed, as they gathered their few things and prepared to leave. "At least they won't be trying to kill me, too. I'm invisible." She pirouetted in front of Nick. "Do I look invisible to you?"

Nick smiled, but she thought he looked strained, his smile a bit forced. She wrapped her arms around him in a warm hug. "Don't worry, Nick. Once we turn in the car you can disappear, too. We'll be safe then."

Before they left, Nick called Oscar in Amsterdam to warn him not to discuss what he had found in the Vermeer paint sample. But he had gone out and no one knew when to expect him back. Nick said he'd call again later. He also called Ben Johnson and left a message telling him about the kauri resin in the Vermeer and the break-in at Oscar's lab. He asked him to call the police art squad in London to inform them right away.

When he hung up, Jerry asked, "Shouldn't we try calling Interpol or something? If the painting is already in New York, then won't they be the ones to handle things?"

"Ben knows the people in London. It'll be faster for him. They'll contact the art squad in New York. It'll take too long for me to get hold of the right people there and to convince them to act."

As they drove along the winding road back to Ventimiglia, they discussed how they would manage without Nick using his credit cards; they could not afford to leave an electronic trail of his whereabouts. The money Jerry had would not get them very far. Nick reasoned that he could be traced to Nice quite easily already. One more piece of evidence in the form of a bank withdrawal would not hurt, as long as the trail went cold in Nice.

Jerry had been voluble and excited as they planned their next move. She was feeling so much better. The shock of losing her loft and almost losing her life was wearing off. The fact that the Vermeer was a fake had barely sunk in. She couldn't help feeling positive when she was with Nick. Must be the hormones, she was thinking dryly when she was struck by another thought. Her good humour evaporated. "What about Carol? Do you think she's safe? Andrew knows how close she is to me. Could he think she knows too much as well?"

Nick, his eyes on the road, answered, "You'd better call her now, Jerry."

She woke her up, it was still very early in the morning in Toronto. Carol became increasingly alert as Jerry explained what had happened.

"I'll take the cats and go up north to the cottage right away. I was going to go up tomorrow anyway."

"Take cash, don't use your credit card. Call me when you get there!" Jerry shouted the last bit, the reception was getting poor. Carol's response was broken up and the line went dead.

"How can Carol call you? She won't know your number, you haven't even rented the phone yet," said Nick.

"Damn. You're right. And I just realized she can't call me any-way — there is no phone at her cottage, and her cellphone won't work up there."

Jerry sat lost in worry and concentration. She was still wear-ing Nick's T-shirt and Carol's slacks. Her feet were sticky and hot in Carol's running shoes and she promised herself that the very first thing she'd do after this painting business was cleared up was go shopping for sandals.

They arrived at the airport just after noon. Nick drove the car into short-term parking directly across from the entrance.

"Nick, this is only for five-minute parking. Why don't we go to the rental section?"

"Let's leave it here. I'm really not feeling very comfortable at the moment. We'd have to walk a lot farther from the rental section and frankly, I know this sounds paranoid, I just want to get rid of this car as fast as possible."

Jerry gave herself a shake. Of course Nick was right, this was hardly the time to be fussing about minutia. Funny how in the middle of a crisis, the normal habitual things assert themselves. At this point, who cared if the car got towed. That would be the least of their worries.

They decided it would be best not to be seen together. Nick went on to the rental counter while Jerry hung back, pretending to browse in a nearby shop selling wines and cheeses from the region. If Nick was going to disappear, there shouldn't be any way to connect him with her. As soon as he was finished, she would saunter in and rent another car from a different company.

She chose some cheese and crackers thinking they would need a snack as soon as they were on the road again. As she went to pay, she felt for her change-purse in her bag and her hands closed on a set of keys. Oh dear, she thought, I forgot that I still have the second set for the rental. She got her change from the clerk, and glanced over at Nick.

Two rather scruffy men were standing very close on either side of him while he waited his turn at the desk. One of them leaned over and said something to him. Nick stiffened and looked around quickly. He said something to the rental clerk who nodded, and then he and his companions turned away from the counter and started to move towards her. Except for Nick's face, which had turned red with fury, it didn't look like anything out of the ordinary was happening, just three men walking in the airport.

"What the hell ...," started Jerry as she watched them approaching. Then it dawned on her, these were no friends of his. Nick was being taken somewhere against his will.

Her heart was beating wildly, every nerve in her body

alight with fear. She thought she must be sending out some extraordinarily powerful distress signal that would be obvious to the two men, but so far neither seemed to be aware of her. It took every fibre of self-control to force her body to turn away and to walk calmly ahead of them towards the entrance. Once outside, she walked slowly to the car, got in, and started the engine. The driver's seat was back as far as possible to accommodate Nick's long legs. She was trying to get it to move forward, yanking at the metal lever under the seat while simultaneously watching out for Nick and the men who had not been far behind her. Suddenly the seat let go and she shot forward. She quickly looked up and saw them in the rear-view mirror. Surely they must have noticed her? But no, they never even glanced in her direction.

The three of them got into a car just two down from where she was, one man in the driver's seat and Nick and the other man in the rear. They backed out, with Jerry following almost immediately. She stayed close behind them as they negotiated the airport exit lanes and pulled into La Promenade des Anglais, the main avenue outside the airport.

Jerry let another car get in between so that it would not be obvious that she was following them. They were headed out to the autoroute where she and Nick had just come in. She mustn't lose that car! She tried to memorize their licence plate, but kept tripping over the long string of numbers. Fishing into her handbag, she pulled out a pen and paper. She held the paper down on the centre of the steering wheel and wrote the numbers as she drove, a skill at which she was singularly adept. She was always recording the names of books or music she heard on the car radio on scraps of paper that would float around in her handbag until they mysteriously disappeared. Jerry's mind was drifting — what ever happened to all those little pieces of paper that vanished in the depths of her voluminous handbags? Suddenly she caught sight of what was ahead and was hit with an electric chill.

"Damn! That's all I need — a bloody toll booth!" she wailed. More fishing in her handbag to find her change-purse, but she was not having much luck. Finally she managed to gather a few coins. She saw them up ahead, pulling into a correct-change lane. She was frantic, what if she got held up? They would be long gone before she had sorted out the money. Where was the stupid sign to tell her how much she would need? She took a chance and chose a correct-change lane, too, praying she had enough. She tossed all the coins she had at the basket and rocked in her seat with anxiety, watching the other car pulling out of the toll lane beside her. The bar in front of her lifted. As she started forward, she heard change falling down the machine's metal chute. She leaned over and grabbed what she could, then tore off after them.

She was vaguely aware that panic was making her light headed and giddy. She had barely regained her lane when she saw their car disappearing down the exit for Ventimiglia, just ahead. It was the same exit that she and Nick had taken the day before. She quickly swerved into the exit remembering that there was another toll booth to negotiate when she came off the ramp, this time in Italy. She fumbled for bills worried that the booth wouldn't take her French money, but luck was with her, she had no trouble getting through and keeping up with them.

It was when she glanced down at the speedometer that she noticed the gas gauge. "Of course, it's almost empty," she said out loud to herself. "It figures."

Jerry followed at a discreet distance as they proceeded through heavy traffic in Ventimiglia. The car headed out of town in the direction of Dolceacqua and back up the same road that she and Nick had come down earlier that day. Just as she congratulated herself on the ease with which she was following them, a yellow light on the dashboard flashed on: the low-gas warning. There was no question of stopping, she would lose them. She just had to hope they would stop somewhere before the gas ran out. The tension was giving her a headache. She became obsessed with the steady little yellow light.

Jerry slowed and let a few more cars get ahead of her on the narrow road, hoping to use less gas, but realizing it probably would not make that much difference. They drove on and on, until she was at the point of screaming. She rounded yet another corner, then saw them turning off into Dolceacqua. Her engine purring along in defiance of the warning light, she followed them across the modern bridge into the piazza in front of a large ornate church at the foot of the medieval town.

The men got out of the car and walked Nick up through an arched stone passageway into the town. Jerry jumped out of her car and followed. The passageway led on to a cobblestoned street where there was only foot traffic. No cars could pass through: there was barely room for the three men to walk abreast. Tiny passageways ran off from the main street and wound ever upwards; it looked as though time had ground to a standstill about three hundred years ago. She saw the men take a right and followed behind. There were plenty of people around, a mix of locals and tourists, so she was not afraid of being noticed.

They stopped on Via Castello, in front of an old wooden door. Jerry hung back. With all the dark entrances to various passageways, there were lots of nooks and crannies from which to watch and not be seen. One of the men took out some keys and opened the door. Nick planted his feet firmly and tried to resist entering, but the other man gave him a sharp shove and, in an instant, they were inside and the door was shut.

Jerry waited in the shadows for what felt like a very long time. Finally the two men came out, locked the door, and retraced their steps down the street towards the piazza.

What should she do? Clearly Nick was still inside, but if she left to go for the police, by the time she found them and convinced them to come here, the men could have moved him. She refused to think about what else could happen or might already have happened.

Just then a woman walked by carrying plastic bags full of groceries; she looked like a local.

"Scusi, signora." Jerry started, then broke into English, "Do you know who lives here? Connaissez-vous qui habit ici?" She tried in her faltering French.

"Personne, signorina," the woman answered. "Nobody lives ... is for sale, questa casa. You want?"

"Oh, yes. I would love to see inside," said Jerry genuinely.

"You go, agenzia immobiliare," replied the woman. She started to give directions in a mixture of Italian and French, pointing down the street behind her. Jerry understood *ponte* and assumed she meant the old stone bridge. She was feeling quite confused when another woman came by and was enlisted to help.

Fortunately she spoke more English, and between the two of them, with a lot of excited gesticulations and repeated references to the *ponte*, Jerry finally had some sense of what they were saying. She gathered that the real estate agent was located in a small street immediately to the left when she crossed the bridge. With a warm *gracia mille,* she sped away, flying down the narrow streets, her pent-up energy finally having some outlet.

She arrived to find the real estate agent in the process of locking her door and leaving for lunch. After ascertaining that the agent spoke some English, Jerry asked whether she could view the house on Via Castello. The woman looked at her watch and frowned, obviously not pleased to be interrupted on her way out. She suggested that Jerry come back at three o'clock. Jerry's heart sank. That could easily be too late: the men could have come back by then. She tried again, "I'm sorry, signora, but I have another appointment then. I can only see it now. Is that possible?" She tried hard not to allow any hint of her anxiety to creep into her voice.

The real estate agent sighed, looked thoroughly disgruntled, and reopened the door. "I will get the key, but I won't give you a long time to look; it's better to make an appointment," she growled.

They walked back towards Via Castello at what felt like a maddingly slow pace to Jerry, who was buzzing with nervous energy and worry. If this woman senses how tense I am right now she is really going to wonder, she thought to herself.

Finally they reached the house. If she hadn't just seen the door opened and Nick shoved through, she wouldn't have believed anyone had been inside this century. The façade of the building was ancient: stones jutted out at all angles and the mortar looked badly in need of repointing. There was a half-hearted whitewash around the perimeter of the door which did not quite cover countless layers of old whitewash below. As the agent sorted through a ring of keys, a grimy black and white cat milled around their feet. When the huge wooden door swung open the cat made a dash for the interior. The agent, a portly middle-aged woman, moved even faster than the cat and caught it with her foot, pushing it surprisingly gently back out on the street, admonishing

Jerry to take care not to let it back in.

They stepped inside. In front of them was a small landing. Steep stone steps took them up to a second tiny landing in front of a well-proportioned room straight ahead. The room had a high arched ceiling and was utterly bare. A single window at the back let in enough light to see that no one had lived there for a very long time. The plaster was peeling, the floor was unswept cement. Two cobweb-covered wooden doors that looked positively medieval were partially closed over a cupboard half-way down the left wall. Only partially closed, because the bottom half of one of the doors was entirely eaten away, and the top left was also missing, presumably devoured by generations of hungry woodworm.

"Interesting," said Jerry, surveying the room. She made a quick check of the cupboard, but it was only as deep as a window-well, which is what it had been in the past; now it was a bricked-up window made into a cupboard. The real estate agent pointed to the floor, which sloped steeply towards the far left corner of the room where there was some type of drain. She must have felt obliged to give Jerry the full tour, because she explained in a rehearsed manner that this floor was originally the roof of the house. It had been sloped to allow rain to run off. As generations went by and the family fortunes improved, further floors had been built on top. Jerry nodded quickly and tried to appear fascinated, although she was having trouble focusing on anything but the screaming desire to get to the rest of the house.

They continued into the next room to the right, which had once been a kitchen. The massive fireplace still held remnants of a wood fire, and there was a large stone dry-sink in front of a tall narrow window, looking out into a window-well shared by other houses. This room was also empty. Jerry began to realize that the house was a relic of another age. It had never been brought into the twentieth century; there was no running water. In the kitchen was a single electric bulb that ran off a small wire, which disappeared down the stairs. That appeared to be the total extent of the electricity.

The agent led the way to the next floor. They climbed more steep stone steps in a stairwell lit only from a window with no glass and a rotting wooden frame. Jerry's tension was mounting.

She was trying to prepare herself for the sight of Nick. They had been in here with him for a while. Had he been beaten? They must have tied him up ... She walked through the two empty rooms on the next floor, which were similar in size and condition to the ones below, then nodded to the agent who led her up another set of stairs. She found herself at the top of the house, with three more empty rooms. Where the hell is he! she thought frantically. I'm running out of rooms!

After her lecture on the sloping floor, the agent had lapsed into silence, obviously just going through the motions and eager for her lunch. On the top floor, she had stayed where she was near the stairs while Jerry had quickly checked the rest of the rooms. When Jerry was through, the women turned to go back down. Jerry pointed to another set of stairs and asked, "Isn't there another floor?"

"The roof," said the agent, not moving.

"Can I see it?" she asked, and sensing the agent's reluctance, added, "I'm thinking of a terrace, perhaps the roof can be made into a terrace."

The agent's shoulders drooped, and she started to climb the last set of stairs to the roof. They came out into a kind of lean-to. There was a sloping ceiling of tiles, supported by crude stone walls. Outside was a flat roof. There was absolutely nothing, except a small wooden hut directly behind the agent. It could just about accommodate a man.

"What is that?" asked Jerry pointing at the wooden structure.

"Birdhouse. Pigeons," she replied, obviously not interested in pursuing the subject.

"Oh really!" said Jerry realizing that was why the cat had been so keen to get in. It looked like the only bit of the whole house that had seen any recent use.

"May I see inside it?"

The agent obstinately stood her ground, but after a long moment while they stared each other down, she abruptly moved aside and Jerry dove for the door, a little hastily, she realized as she swung it open.

Empty.

"Damn," Jerry muttered under her breath. He isn't here.

They must have come back for him while I was getting the real estate agent. I should never have left — what a fool I am, she said to herself savagely.

Jerry mutely followed the agent back down the stairs, caught up in her own thoughts. She was feeling more and more frantic about what to do next. Just as they were starting down the last set of stairs leading to the front entrance, she caught sight of a door sunk into the wall on the right side. It had been hidden by the front door when they had come in.

"Where does that door lead to?" She called out, hearing an edge to her voice she had been trying so hard not to reveal. She was sure that the agent knew something peculiar was going on.

"La cave, the wine cellar."

"Can I see it?"

"It's not for sale. The owners of the house have decided to keep it. They have a separate entrance to it off the street."

Momentarily nonplussed, Jerry searched for a rationale to get the estate agent to open the door. That had to be where they put Nick. She slowed her descent down the stairs, then asked, "Do you have a key?"

"Yes, but it's not for sale. I told you."

Jerry began hesitantly, "If I want to buy this house, I will need to see the foundations and I expect that involves the wine cellar. It would save such a lot of time and bother if you would just let me see it now," she said, in what she hoped was a firm and reasonable voice.

The agent did not answer, her back was rigid. As she started to open the front door, it was clear that she had no intention of showing her the wine cellar. Jerry was wildly contemplating wrestling her to the ground for the key, when the black and white cat flew in the partly opened door and disappeared underneath the wine-cellar door, which had been eaten away at the bottom, leaving ample room for a cat to find easy access.

The agent swore under her breath, and started sorting through her keys. Jerry exhaled then allowed herself a deep breath. Thank god for that cat.

As the door swung open, the first thing that met their eyes in the dim interior was a man slumped on the floor. Jerry could no longer control herself, she cried out to Nick and rushed passed the agent who stood astonished in the doorway repeating "Dio mio" and patting her heart. Jerry was urgently trying to cut the nylon cord around his wrists with a pair of ridiculously small scissors from her Swiss Army knife. She heard the agent say something about *polizia* and then she was gone. Meanwhile Jerry cut his hands free from the cord and as Nick started to tear off the tape over his mouth, she went to work on his ankles, which had also been bound. Fortunately the nylon wasn't thick so it was relatively easy to cut through. Moments later, she was helping him to his feet. He staggered as the circulation slowly returned to his legs.

"Hurry, Nick. We've got to get out of here fast, before the police arrive. If they find us, we'll be stuck in endless questions. In the meantime, those men could be back any minute," she said with urgency. "Are you hurt, did they hurt you?" she added, frantically patting him all over.

"I'm all right, Jerry. Don't worry, let's just go."

Nick leaned heavily on Jerry's slender shoulders as they struggled up the cellar stairs and into the street. He gradually got the feeling back in his legs, and was growing stronger by the moment. Soon he no longer needed her support and they rushed down the street and through the arched passageway into the piazza, clambering into the Citroën. As Jerry started the engine, the little yellow light on the dash flashed into life.

"I forgot! We're almost out of gas. So much for the instant getaway," she mourned.

Nick laughed and shook his head. He reached over and took her hand from the steering wheel and gave it a squeeze. "Don't worry, Jerry. You're brilliant to have rescued me. I couldn't believe it when I heard your voice in the hallway. Then when you kept going up the stairs and it seemed like you wouldn't find me I was beside myself. Those two were very mean characters. I'm not sure how much longer I would have lasted if they'd returned before you found me."

"How are we going to get out of here without gas? There can't be much left, that light was on practically the whole way from Ventimiglia," she said as she backed up the car and turned it around to face the modern bridge which led out of the piazza.

"There's bound to be a station somewhere ahead. If it runs out on the way, we'll just walk."

"Oh, Christ, Nick, they're back! Get down!" she shouted as she saw the two men in their car coming towards them over the bridge. Nick slumped down in his seat. Jerry gripped the steering wheel and waited for them to clear the bridge before she zoomed forward and past them. She had no idea if they saw her or Nick. "Just get us across the bridge," she pleaded with the car. She made a right as soon as they were over the bridge, and headed towards the centre of the modern part of Dolceacqua. The car was no longer running smoothly and she knew they were not going to get very far. Once the men had been to the house they would be back and looking for him. They might even know this car; they could have traced him through the rental in the first place.

Acting on impulse, she wrenched the car to the left, turning down a small crooked laneway. She had just managed to get out of sight of the main street before the car, chugging and bucking, finally came to a complete halt. They jumped out, quickly pushing it to one side. No point in drawing any more attention to themselves by leaving it in the middle of the street. Then they took off at a run. Nick suggested that they look for a gas station.

"I think we should try and get another car somehow; it's too risky to use that one," she answered.

Slowing down to a quick walk, they left the maze of small back laneways and found themselves on another main street. It was just after two-thirty and the shops were shut fast for the long Italian lunch break. Jerry realized that she was extraordinarily thirsty and hungry.

"I know this sounds daft," she said, "but I think we should just find some small restaurant and eat something."

Nick nodded, it made sense. They wouldn't be able to find a new rental car until the shops opened again. It was highly un-likely that the men would find him or even think to look for him in a restaurant. People running from danger don't usually stop for a meal. They saw a small trattoria ahead that would do perfectly. Jerry had her chance to freshen up and even managed to wash her face. She looked down ruefully at what was now her all-purpose black T-shirt, wishing she could have a change of clothes. No time for that now.

They sat at a table in the back, facing the door, ever watchful. They ordered the daily special, starting with antipasto, followed by pasta then a meat dish with vegetables. They polished off a full bottle of sparkling water and ordered a second.

Their waiter informed them that there was no car rental agency in Dolceacqua, they would have to make their way back to Ventimiglia. Fortunately the waiter's brother-in-law drove a taxi. By the time they had paid their bill, he was waiting outside to take them into the larger town. The trip was uneventful, though both Jerry and Nick spent the entire journey in a tense silence as they scanned the cars on their way for any sign of the two men. They were finally deposited at the rental agency, and Jerry made arrangements for a small red Renault.

"Well," said Jerry as she got into the driver's seat, "where to now?"

"I've been thinking about that. What about going to Nice? It's big, we can find a hotel, and then we can phone Ben from our room, rather than trying to manage from some call box on the street. I hope he got my message."

"Good, by the time we get there and get a room, it'll be around five. That's still only four in London, so if we need to call the people ourselves, they'll still be in the office."

Getting out of Ventimiglia was less difficult than it had been that morning. This time they were both alert to the signs and familiar with the convoluted maze of on-ramps leading to the autoroute.

"When were they planning to auction the Vermeer?" asked Nick when they were finally heading towards Nice.

"I'm not sure. I thought it would be the end of this week. I have to say it was the last thing on my mind before I left Canada," she answered.

"Poor Jerry. It's been pretty crazy for you, hasn't it?" he replied. "Don't worry. Once the police know about this, they'll investigate. I imagine they usually act pretty quickly when they have a tip. Ben has probably contacted them already. We're doing fine now." He reached over to pat her thigh reassuringly, and she gave his hand a quick squeeze in response.

The Renault was much smaller than the Citroën. At full speed on the busy autoroute, it didn't feel particularly safe. This was a bad stretch of highway: other cars raced past, trucks formed long convoys, and they were buffeted by the winds on exposed parts of the road. As well, there were many long tunnels through the mountains, which meant they were going from intense bright sunlight into sudden darkness. It always took a few moments for their eyes to adjust, then when they were feeling comfortable, they were hit with full sun again. Jerry had a pair of sunglasses in her bag, which she put on, but Nick's were with his things in the car the two men had been driving.

"Nick, what about checking into the hotel? Should we be seen together?"

"Right ...," he answered slowly, gathering his thoughts. "That's a good point. I'll wait for you somewhere then you can tell me the room number, and I'll come up separately. No point in taking any chances."

They decided to choose a large hotel, hoping for more anonymity. When they reached Nice, Nick got out of the car a block from the Hotel Negresco along La Promenade des Anglais. Jerry drove on to the hotel, leaving the car with the valet. They had arranged to see each other in the lobby, a huge room with a display of modern sculptures and a selection of boutiques.

Jerry checked in without incident, then proceeded to the lobby. Nick appeared to be studying one of the sculptures. As she passed she whispered the room number. He inclined his head ever so slightly in response. Soon after she found the room and let herself in, there was a knock on the door; she swung it open to let Nick in.

He sat on the edge of the sumptuous bed and immediately began dialling Ben. Jerry hovered nearby, unable to relax until she knew their message had been passed on to the proper authorities. During the drive into Nice, she and Nick had discussed their situation at length. They decided that once the painting was exposed as a fraud, the threat to their lives, well, to Nick's anyway, since she didn't currently have one, would be over. Once their information was out and the sale was stopped, they should be safe.

There was no answer at Ben's. Nick got through to Interpol headquarters in Lyons and discovered he would have to phone the FBI art squad in New York. He recommended dialling. Jerry crossed the luxurious carpet and perched on the edge of a chair in the corner of the room, watching him. He had to go through three different individuals until he finally found the right person. Nick explained the situation briefly, then as Jerry fidgeted, she heard him respond.

"Yes, the Vermeer. It's coming from Toronto to be auctioned this week ... yes, I'll wait." He looked over at Jerry. "They're calling the auction house right now."

She raised her eyebrows, he shrugged, started to say something to her, then spoke into the phone. "What? Oh, no. Are you sure? We thought it would be later this week," he said, his voice raised in concern. Jerry watched intently, trying to understand what was happening.

"Yes. Three female figures, yes. This morning ... well ..." Nick exhaled a long sigh. "Then there is nothing you can do?" he asked without hope. "Yes, yes ... I understand ... yes, I will make a full report. Thank you." He replaced the handset with an air of weary resignation.

Jerry sprang to her feet, "What happened, Nick?" she demanded.

"It was auctioned off this morning. It's gone. That's it."

"What do you mean 'That's it'!" she exclaimed. "It's still a fake! What about the new owner? He should be notified. They can still go after it — the auction house just sold him a fake!"

Nick walked over to Jerry. He gently put his hands on her the shoulders, and looked into her eyes. "Jerry, listen. It went to a major institution — a public gallery. The police won't investigate unless the new owner requests them to."

Jerry put her hands up onto his arms, squeezing him as she continued earnestly, "When we tell the new owners they've just bought a fake, they'll ask the police to investigate."

Nick dropped his arms and walked over to the bed, where he again sat on the edge. "It just doesn't work that way. I'm so sorry."

Jerry sank slowly back into her chair. She stared across at him and said quietly, "I don't understand."

"When a large institution makes a new acquisition like this, there'll be a huge splash in the media. There's a great deal of prestige in purchasing a major painting, huge amounts of public money are involved. No one wants the embarrassment of discovering it's a fake. That means their judgement was off; it questions their expertise. Large institutions don't admit to mistakes like this, Jerry. The last thing the new owners want is an investigation that could make them look bad."

"But surely it's the auction house that's looking bad and is responsible?"

"Only as long as the painting is with them; then they are obliged to deal with any allegations of fraud. Once it's sold, it's no longer their problem."

Jerry rubbed her forehead and pushed her hair back off her face. She tried again to reason with what Nick was telling her. "Sometimes a large gallery will admit when they have a questionable piece. Look at the Mauritshuis in The Hague. I was just reading about how they have recently re-attributed one of their most prized Rembrandts, *The Self-Portrait with Gorget*. Now they're saying it is by one of his students."

He looked up with a wry smile. "Yes, I remember that one. Questions were raised about its attribution to Rembrandt and then they went public with new information which showed theirs was a copy and the original was in Nuremberg."

"Well?" said Jerry hopefully. "See, they do admit mistakes."

"First of all, the painting was already in their permanent collection — it had been acquired god knows when — so no one's reputation was riding on its attribution. Second, it was a copy made by one of his students, not a fake. No one individual at the Gallery would lose face admitting that the painting was not by Rembrandt; no one's head was going to roll. And third, and most telling in my opinion, from the time doubts were first raised, until a proper analytical investigation took place, *eight years* went by, Jerry."

Jerry looked at him, silent, absorbing the information.

Nick continued. "Most of the time, when questions are raised about a piece, or new information arises, galleries just quietly change the attribution. One day, a painting is 'by' Rubens, the next day, the label says, 'attributed to.' Slight change of wording. Most people don't even notice. And, as I'm sure you know, there are still many more paintings in galleries whose attributions are highly questionable, and they haven't had their labels changed."

Jerry nodded unhappily. She knew he was right, there were countless museums proudly displaying their valuable old master paintings. Many professionals seriously doubted these attributions, but few were willing to come forward. Even the big blockbuster exhibitions had their embarrassing pieces.

"So the new owner of the so-called Vermeer will let the fanfare surrounding its acquisition die down, and then maybe, one day, in eight to ten years, if we keep badgering them, they'll do some tests and quietly change the label. That's what you're telling me," she said, her voice heavy with disappointment.

"It's the most-likely scenario. I doubt we would be able to get anywhere for at least a few years. And by then, of course, the trail will be quite cold. And don't forget, Andrew cannot be accused of fraud without more evidence than we have now. He just bought an old painting on behalf of a client, and that painting turned out to have a Vermeer underneath it. He's as clean as can be."

"And we can't tie him to the attempt on my life, or to your kidnapping, or to the break-in at Oscar's lab?"

"Well, *we* can't. Perhaps a proper investigator could. But who will investigate?"

"Damn! This is frustrating!" exclaimed Jerry, on the edge of tears. "After all we've been put through, there's nothing at all we can do about it!"

Nick walked over to her, pulled her up out of the chair and held her closely.

"We're both safe, Jerry," he said quietly, trying to reassure her. "It could've been worse. I doubt they care about us now. They know we can't do them any more damage."

She allowed herself to be led over to the bed. Nick and she lay together on top of the covers. As she began to relax in the circle of his arms, she felt a wave of pure exhaustion. Soon she drifted off to sleep, and so did Nick who was just as tired.

A few hours later Jerry got up to take a shower. As she shampooed her hair in the hot water she started to feel more like herself again. Nick joined her and they soaped each other down. Neither felt like anything more than the reassuring contact they were having. It was enough just to touch each other and to be held.

As Jerry pulled on Nick's black T-shirt and Carol's slacks, she decided she really could not stand wearing these clothes any longer. Nick agreed to take a walk outside with her in search of a shop.

"Do we still need to play cloak and daggers? Shall we leave separately?" she asked as they prepared to go.

"Probably not, I imagine those thugs were only hired to keep me out of the way until the painting was sold. Still, let's not draw attention to ourselves. We can go out at the same time, but we'll act like we aren't together. It will be hard for me to remember not to touch you, though. I can't seem to stop," he added, smiling.

Eventually they found a small boutique that looked inviting. Nick sat down with a newspaper in a café just up the street, while Jerry went shopping. Once inside the store she realized it was very expensive, and the buyers obviously catered to a much older clientele. It was going to be difficult to find anything that suited. Feeling desperate, as there were no other shops nearby, she forced herself to select a pair of trousers, a tailored blouse, a light jacket, and some underwear. The effect, which was very conventional, wasn't her at all, she thought as she studied her reflection in the mirror. She tried to console herself. "Now that I am presumed dead, I'm not myself anymore anyway. So I guess it doesn't matter." She found a pair of open-toed shoes that matched her new look. As she settled the bill, she explained that she would wear the new clothes and take the old ones in a bag.

On her way up the street towards the café, Jerry felt quite self-conscious. She had never considered before how important her clothes were to her sense of self. It felt extremely peculiar to be dressed in a combination of clothes suited to a dowdy but wealthy middle-aged woman. Clean yes, but chic, no. Lint-free though, she thought to herself.

Nick greeted her with a puzzled grin, and she blushed with embarrassment.

"This is all I could find," she shrugged apologetically, feeling even worse.

"You look fine. Don't worry," his eyes appraised her and he smiled gently. "They fit very well you know."

They walked back towards the hotel enjoying the warm evening air. As much as they would have liked to take a leisurely stroll down the boardwalk at the edge of the sea, and to eat outside in one of the many restaurants lining the Promenade, they decided it would be wiser to stay inside and order room service. There was no point in taking any chances.

During dinner, they discussed what to do next. Jerry would call Detective-Sergeant Wiens to let him know what had happened. She could probably catch him before he left the office, it was ten o'clock in Nice, only four p.m. in Toronto.

She reached him easily and poured out her news. When she told him about finding the wrong resin in the Vermeer, she heard a sharp intake of breath. She waited for his response, hoping he would suggest that something might still be done. Not surprisingly, his assessment of the situation was like Nick's. He too considered the case essentially closed.

He promised they would continue to investigate her loft explosion and Andrew's possible role, but they had already run a background check on him and he was completely clean.

"Why don't you get on the next flight to Toronto," he advised. "I'll send a car out to Carol at her cottage to let her know the latest developments. I'd like you both back in the city, at her place where we can keep an eye on you. I'll need you to come in and give me a statement as soon as you can."

As she got off the phone, Jerry felt despondent. She hadn't considered that he might suggest she come back so soon. When would she and Nick be together again? This feeling of empty disappointment was not the way she had imagined things turning out. She could see from Nick's expression that he had already worked out what had to happen next. He reached out to her and she went into his arms.

"You have a lot of things to sort out at home. You'll have to deal with your insurance, and I should get back to Cambridge," he gave her a squeeze. "Get your affairs settled, and then let's have a proper vacation together in England."

They made love with a sadness and poignancy new to their

relationship. After experiencing so much together, the parting the next day would be difficult. As much as she wanted to stay, to forget that any of this had happened, and to concentrate on being with him, she realized it did not make sense to prolong her absence from Toronto. There was a lot to do: rising from the dead, for one thing.

Chapter 19

JERRY LET HERSELF INTO CAROL'S APARTMENT laden with bags of new clothes. She was trying to put them down but the roiling mass of Alvin and Tony at her feet made it difficult to find an empty bit of floor. They were still delighted to have her home, even though it had been three days since her return, so she naturally assumed they were presenting her with a particularly effusive greeting. "Honestly, you two, can you just move a bit?" she said, exasperated. But as she straightened up, she realized they weren't frantically greeting her, they were frantic to get out.

"Andrew! What are you doing here?" she cried in alarm, instinctively shrinking back against the door.

As perfectly turned out as ever, Andrew stood in front of her, looking grave.

"Jerry, I'm so glad to see you. I could hardly believe it when I heard you had been killed in the explosion ... and, well ... now here you are!" he finished somewhat lamely.

"How did you get in?" she demanded tersely, still caught off guard.

"Why, Carol let me in of course. She's in the kitchen," he answered mildly, a little perplexed at her response. "I'm anxious to hear how you are and where you've been. Shall we sit in the living room?"

Jerry pulled herself away from the door, and found herself following him automatically. She could hear noises in the kitchen and assumed Carol was preparing something. She chose a seat in a deep wing-backed chair as far away as she could manage from where he was sitting.

He settled down on the corner of the long sofa and took a sip from his drink, then smiled at her, as she sat nervously watching him.

"First of all, I brought you something." He put his glass down and drew something out of his suit pocket. He reached over, offering it to her. "I thought it was the least I could do, after our great success with the Vermeer and that terrible accident at your studio."

Jerry looked at him with distaste: she could see from where she sat that it was a cheque. She didn't move. Andrew held it a fraction longer, then realizing she was not going to take it, he stood up, walked over and put it down in front of her on the coffee table.

She glanced down: it was for $500,000. She looked up at him, still standing by her chair. "Hush money, Andrew?" she said, her voice heavy with repugnance.

He stood rooted to the spot, clearly shocked, and said softly, "What are you talking about, Jerry?"

She put her head back on the chair and looked up at him for a long moment before answering. Then she leaned forward, "You must know I suspect you of trying to have me killed. You must realize that."

As her words sank in, red crept up his throat and infused his face in an angry blush. He shook his head in disbelief. "Jerry, I don't have the faintest idea why you would think that. What motive could I possibly have?" He went back to the couch and sat down.

"Andrew. I know about the Vermeer."

"*What* do you know about it!" he exploded.

"That it's not right ...," she began.

"Where are you getting this? What do you mean 'it's not right'?" he demanded, interrupting her.

This was not going as she had imagined. Ever since the moment they discovered that the Vermeer was a fake, she'd been planning this confrontation with Andrew. But in her mind she was the one in charge, the one to be angry and articulate: Andrew was penitent and remorseful.

"We ... we ... had the medium analyzed ...," she stammered.

"You told me that," he broke in, furious, "and you found some bloody resin in the paint, so what!"

"But we found out it was kauri copal. Kauri resin was not

available before the nineteenth century."

Andrew sprang out of his seat and rounded on her; she shrank back into the chair.

"Who the hell told you that? Nobody can identify resins like that — what are you saying?" His handsome face was suffused with anger, red patches appeared in his cheeks and, she noticed with an odd detachment, that his neck was blotched with red. He may not collect lint, but he sure looks like hell when he's angry, she thought.

She said nothing, and he suddenly seemed to pull himself together. He took a deep breath and sat down again.

"Jerry," he began quietly, "where did you get this information? Was it from Nick?"

"Yes."

"Did you actually see the analytical results yourself?"

"Well, no ..., " she admitted, "but ..."

He broke in, "I don't think you've thought this through very well. Has it ever occurred to you that Nick could have made it up?"

Shocked, Jerry sat up in her chair, grabbing the arms. "Why would he lie to me? That doesn't make any sense!"

"Yes it does. He could've been trying to undermine the credibility of the sale. If he spread enough rumours about the authenticity of the Vermeer in front of the right people, it could have been very damaging to the price it fetched at auction. Very damaging."

Jerry paled. She found herself clutching the arms of the chair.

He continued softly, "So damaging in fact, that the price would have been driven way below its value. Then maybe he or a partner could pick it up themselves at a very reduced price."

She stood up, her face the colour of chalk, her emotions barely suppressed. She spoke in a low even tone: "Get out, Andrew. I will not listen to this."

Andrew's mouth fell open, and he gaped at her in total surprise.

"I mean it, leave right now," she ordered. Somewhere in the back of her mind, it occurred to her that he might refuse. What the hell would she do then? Where was Carol?

He got up from the sofa. She swept the cheque up off the coffee table and presented it to him. Without a word he took it, and turned on his heel. She stood in the living room holding her breath as she heard the front door open, then close. She sank back into her chair, let out a long breath and and burst into tears.

Carol found her there moments later. "I heard everything from the kitchen. I didn't trust myself to be in the room with him, so I waited in there to see what he would do. I had the phone ready. If he had tried anything, I was going to dial emergency. What a scene! Poor you, Jerry, I'm so sorry."

"Why did you let him in?" gasped Jerry as she tried to pull herself together.

"I don't know. I guess I couldn't break through the good manners. It was all very polite and proper, all so innocent. I found myself responding, offering him a drink ... it was like being locked in some play," she said. "If I'd been thinking fast enough, I would have shut the door in his face. But he was in so quickly and talking so normally ... I just ... well, I just went along with him. I couldn't seem to help myself," she finished apologetically.

Jerry smiled up at Carol through her tears and gave her arm a squeeze. She was right. He'd had the same effect on her. After all, he'd manoeuvred her into sitting with him in the living room. If he hadn't made her so furious by offering her that cheque, who knows, they might have been inviting him to stay for dinner.

Carol decided it was time for them to do some serious thinking, and got out a cool bottle of white wine with two long-stemmed glasses.

"So he offered you some money, how much?" asked Carol as she handed Jerry her glass.

"Five hundred thousand."

"Half a million dollars?!" she cried incredulously. "Where is it?"

"I gave it back to him."

"Wow." Carol paused to let this sink in, then, "Why? That's a hell of a lot of money, Jerry. You could really use that. I think he owes it to you, after all you've been through."

"I couldn't accept it, Carol," said Jerry, as though it must be painfully obvious.

"Why not?"

"Carol! If he is as dirty as I think he is, and I accept money from him, then I look pretty damn dirty too, don't I? It would make me look like an accomplice."

Carol shrugged, and took a long sip of wine. "Maybe," she said doubtfully, "but you told me this case isn't going to go anywhere, that it's all over. No one can pin anything on him and no one is going to try to prove the Vermeer's a fake. Can't you just go off into the sunset with your half a million dollars and call it a day?"

"Right," Jerry said, smiling at Carol, knowing she would have reacted the same way.

"That's what should happen, though. After all you've been through over this damn painting, and they get zillions of dollars, it's just not fair!" Carol pronounced and had some more wine. They sat in silence for a while.

"What about Nick? We have to think about what Andrew said. Could Nick be the bad guy?"

"I don't see how ...," started Jerry automatically.

"Let's see ... the first time someone tried to break into your apartment, I was there. The second time, when the painting was stolen ...," she continued, piecing things together, suddenly her eyes lit up and she looked at Jerry in triumph, "you were off in Ottawa rolling around in bed with Nick, weren't you? Isn't the timing rather interesting? You're called away to Ottawa the very weekend the painting is stolen. Could there be a connection?"

Jerry sipped her wine and turned it over in her mind. She had to admit it was quite a coincidence. But the idea that Nick was somehow involved was preposterous. So much so that she found it easy to play along with Carol. It was so ridiculous it was completely unthreatening.

She entered the game, "Okay, what if Nick is behind it all? Why would he be kidnapped in Nice when we took the rental car back?" she asked.

"Um ..." Carol sat back in her chair, put her legs up on the footstool and took another sip of wine. "He set it up to make his story about the Vermeer being faked more convincing to you."

"Right, so he hired two guys to meet him at the airport and fake a kidnapping. They made sure it was easy for me to follow them. Which is true, by the way. It actually was really easy," she admitted. "But," she continued, thinking out loud, "what was the point? If we'd gotten to the police before the painting was sold, and there was further analysis, it wouldn't prove his allegation that the painting was faked, and he would be right back where we started — an authentic Vermeer being auctioned off."

"Unless ...," began Carol, trying to find a way out of the cul de sac Jerry had just presented, "unless he could interfere with the analysis that the police did and somehow intercept the results, or fake them so that it looked like the painting wasn't right."

"Really, Carol, this is just too farfetched. Even if he had an army of scientists in his pocket who would trot out whatever results he wanted, if they proved the Vermeer wasn't authentic, then he would ruin things for himself, too."

"How?"

"Well, having proved it's a fake, he can't turn around to sell it as genuine later, can he? So even if he drives the price down and picks up a cheap Vermeer for himself and his 'partner,' how are they supposed to unload it and make a huge profit?"

"Good point," Carol conceded.

They lapsed into silence for a while, neither able to add anything further. Then Carol sat up and snapped her fingers. "I've got it!"

"Okay, what?" answered Jerry with a lazy smile. The wine was having its effect and she felt mildly anaesthetized.

"What if he never was going to go to the police? Andrew said Nick intended to spread rumours and innuendo that would be damaging enough to keep the bidding low."

"But he phoned them, right in front of me in the hotel. I heard him," answered Jerry.

"That's only what it looked like. He could have been phoning his partner, and faking the call to the police."

Jerry frowned. This no longer felt like such a benign conversation. She squirmed a little in her chair and reached for the wine bottle to refill the glasses. She was silent such a long time that Carol became restless.

Jerry was lost in thought. What if that phone call Nick made when he was sitting on the side of the bed at the Hotel Negresco was all a fabrication? Say he set that up? "Wait a minute, Carol," she said suddenly. "He told me the painting had been auctioned off that morning. He had no need to fake anything then, the whole thing was a *fait accompli*."

"No, Jerry. It just means his plans fell through. He phones his partner and pretends it's the art fraud unit, or whatever, but then his friend tells him the awful news that the painting really was auctioned off. Their attempt to devalue it failed. He has just wasted his time trying to get you on side."

"Damn," breathed Jerry, flopping back into her seat and taking a long drink of wine.

"Okay, then, Carol, who blew up my loft and why?" she countered.

It was Carol's turn to mutter "Damn," and they sat back in companionable silence.

Chapter 20

As the days passed, Carol and Jerry returned to this theme, worrying over the details, inventing plausible explanations, and sharing their theories. Meanwhile, Jerry met with the insurance company, with her lawyer, with Detective-Sergeant Wiens, and tried to weave the threads of her life back into something that made sense again. She managed to shut off the idea of Nick's possible culpability in one compartment of her brain, while other parts continued to adore him and respond to his daily emails.

Although her insurance would cover the rent for a modest apartment while she waited for the full settlement, she was more comfortable staying with Carol, who in turn was perfectly happy to have her there. The weather was getting warmer every day. While she was away in Nice, the trees in Toronto had done their yearly overnight burst into full leaf, which Jerry always felt she missed even when she was there. Happens every year, she marvelled to herself, as she accompanied Alvin and Tony on one of their mid-morning walks in the ravine. One moment it's buds, the next moment it's a full summer forest. What a contrast from spring in England, she reflected. There it all starts in February and goes on for weeks. Various shrubs and trees each sprouting and unfurling their leaves one after another in some beautifully orchestrated movement towards full summer. In Toronto, it all happens in a matter of days.

She came back to the apartment with the cats, feeling refreshed from their walk. Carol was home from work with a nasty head cold and met them at the door.

"Jerry, you got a call from England. The South Kensington Museum, it sounded very official. Here's the number. They wanted you to phone back as soon as possible." Jerry let the cats out of their carriers, and checked her watch. It was just before noon, five in the evening in London; someone might still be there. She'd give it a try. She went into the kitchen to use the phone, while Carol sat at the table in her bathrobe, waiting to hear the news.

"Ah. Ms. McPherson. Thank you for calling back today. I'm with the personnel department," said a warm female voice. "We'd like to offer you the position of assistant restorer. We'll need your response as soon as possible. Do you need time to think about it?"

"Oh ... No ... Not at all. I'm delighted! I'll be very happy to accept the position."

"Good. I must warn you, however, that we'll need to apply for a work visa for you, and that usually takes some time."

"How much time?" she asked.

"It can take weeks, even months. I'm sorry. But it's out of our control once we make the application."

"Do I need to do anything at this point?"

"Yes, you must send us your birth certificate ..."

Jerry grabbed a pen and took down the list of forms she would need to provide. It was difficult to pay attention. What a break! This is what she had barely dared to hope for. A permanent job, with a fabulous collection. In London — in England. Near Nick! Carol was up and dancing in her robe as Jerry hung up the phone. They swirled around the kitchen together, laughing and shouting.

Jerry settled in to wait for the paperwork to be processed in England. As the days passed, she found herself with time on her hands. She started volunteering in the art gallery's conservation department.

One weekend a few weeks after Jerry had received the news from the museum in London, Carol suggested they take the cats and drive up to her cottage. They decided to make it a long week-end and piled the car with provisions in anticipation of a few days in the wilderness. Alvin and Tony seemed well aware of the plans, and were both eager to get into their carriers.

The car journey took hours, but it was a beautiful sunny Friday in June with nothing ahead but relaxation, so they enjoyed themselves. Once off the main highways and onto the winding gravel roads that took them farther from civilization, they felt the immense natural forest enveloping them. Jerry opened her window to let the smell of pine permeate the car.

"What a wonderful scent. I always forget how much fresher the air is outside the city, and how much I miss the resinous smell of the woods. It's simply glorious, isn't it?" she said.

Alvin lay curled up on her lap, totally at ease in the car. Tony was sound asleep in the back seat. They thought nothing of a long trip like this. Since they had all moved in with Carol, Alvin and Tony seemed to have largely forgotten their differences, and were much more comfortable in each other's company. It was a great relief not to have to referee between constant eruptions and disputes. Carol was particularly pleased with this development. She had never quite accepted their angry outbursts as posturing, and was always worrying it would escalate until one of them did serious damage to the other. Jerry was much more sanguine about the rivalry, but she too was glad they were getting along better now, especially while they were all staying with Carol.

Jerry sat in the car, the full sun filtering through the trees, enjoying the woods and the prospect of a break at the cottage. Her plans for England were all in place, her future was taking shape; if only the past were less of mystery.

❦

The next day after lunch, lounging in the cottage's screened-in porch with their drinks beside them and the brilliant green forest crowding out the scene of the lake before them, they fell back into what had become a familiar pastime.

"Where were we? Let's go back to Nick being the bad guy," said Carol.

"I don't see why you feel you have to pick on him all the time. Andrew makes a much better villain in my opinion. He's much too perfect with his English public school accent, those expensive clothes and magazine-model looks. There has *got* to be something wrong."

"But he was so shocked when you confronted him. He sounded genuinely aghast at your accusations."

"It's true, he was very convincing, wasn't he?" agreed Jerry.

"You realize that there's someone we haven't considered properly in all of this, don't you?"

"Who? Detective-Sergeant Wiens?" They collapsed in a fit of laughter. The idea of the ever-so-bureaucratic Detective-Sergeant being in any way connected with wrongdoing tickled them enormously.

"Seriously, Carol, who are we leaving out?" asked Jerry after she'd caught her breath.

"The owner, of course. The mystery man."

"Or woman," added Jerry. "It's true, you know. We've never thought about the *owner*," she said, enunciating the word with the same mix of deference and pomposity that Andrew always managed to infuse it with. "Do you think he or she really exists?"

"Andrew may dress well, but I doubt he has the finances to pick up the occasional old master. Your work alone on that painting would have set the owner back a lot, that is, if it hadn't paid off so well. Now your bill will seem like peanuts."

"True, and I still haven't been paid, come to think of it."

"Well, if you go around tossing back cheques for five-hundred thou ..."

Jerry smiled at her. They sipped their wine, mulling over the information they had gleaned so far.

"Okay, lets assume that your faith in Nick is well-founded, and the Vermeer is a fake after all," said Carol. "Whoever set that up had to know a lot about restoration and about painting materials. I can't see your average art historian knowing enough about either of those things to pull it off with the attention to detail that we saw. And an artist, who might well have the skill to do the painting, would not normally know enough about restoration to have made it as convincing as it was."

"You're right," agreed Jerry. "First of all there was the acrylic overpaint. I remember being puzzled as I took it off that it was not hiding any damage or abrasion in the paint below. I ended up agreeing with Professor Johnson who suggested that it was just there to change the composition; but that never felt completely right."

"So let's assume that the acrylic overpaint was there to obscure the first painting, the van Ruisdael-style landscape. The overpaint made it look more important than it was by allowing only a suggestion of the quality of the painting underneath to show through. That way it was more difficult to judge. And, by showing that the 'van Ruisdael' had been worked on, even if it appeared to be pretty much hack-work, it indicated that someone considered it important enough to be worth restoring."

"Yes," agreed Jerry thoughtfully. "A clever device. Old paintings often have evidence of at least two or three campaigns of restoration, don't they? Remember that seventeenth-century piece we worked on at school? It had been restored four different times; it was like doing archeology to uncover the original."

Carol nodded. "And as we went down, layer by layer, we could see that each restorer had used completely different materials. The first layer on top was badly painted, too, wasn't it? Just like on the 'van Ruisdael.' But the oldest layers of restoration were beautifully done. Remember?" She cut a piece of cheese and had another sip of wine.

"So," continued Carol, "if we accept the premise that the 'van Ruisdael' was only made to look like it was done in the nineteenth century, and that it and the Vermeer underneath were both faked recently, then someone was playing to an audience which had to include another restorer. Who else would appreciate this level of so-called authenticity?"

"That's Nick's idea, too. He thought it was set up deliberately to convince a restorer that this was a bona fide old painting. That way, the restoration history would provide a kind of provenance. The Vermeer had been painted over completely by another image, presumably to allow it to be smuggled out of the country without suspicion. The painting over the Vermeer was made to look nineteenth century, so that it would be old enough to have been repaired itself and painted over during a later 'restoration.'"

"Right, not only would the faker then have a professional restorer on hand to testify to its authenticity, but there would be all the careful documentation, pigment analysis, and cross-sections that go along with the restoration treatment — adding even more weight to the impression of its authenticity."

"Then, at the last minute, in come the art experts who only have to agree that the painting fits stylistically within the attribution," continued Jerry. "Few art historians would be in a position to evaluate the validity of the restoration evidence and the analysis. They would be happy to defer to the opinion of the restorer for that, just as the restorer relies on them for their connoisseurship and knowledge of art history. Neither looks too critically at the other, and in this case, what is missing in one area is made up in the other."

"I agree," said Carol. "If there was any hesitation about the brushwork the art expert would be swayed by the scientific evidence."

"And any lingering doubts about the physical evidence, like the acrylic overpaint covering perfectly healthy-looking paint below, would be lost in the weight of opinion based on the final image and the likelihood of its being original," finished Jerry.

Carol whistled slowly. "Clever. Very clever."

"Whoever did this must know the business inside out."

Carol sipped her wine. "It's a pretty small field, Jerry. Who do you think could have done this? Who knows that much about materials and restoration and is talented enough to paint such a convincing Vermeer?"

Jerry shrugged. "It's not that difficult to think of people with the right knowledge, but as for the talent, no one ever sees that side of a restorer. The better they are at restoration, the more invisible their work is. We don't see much evidence of each other's independent painting ability."

"Okay, so who has that kind of knowledge?" pushed Carol, looking intently at Jerry.

Jerry looked around the room, stalling. Carol waited. The afternoon was warming up rapidly, soon they would find it too hot on the porch to enjoy sitting there. Jerry thought idly of taking the canoe out for a trip around the lake. She listened to the low hum of insects outside and the gentle breeze rustling the leaves. The smell of pine resin was growing stronger, mixed with the smell of the wood from the cabin itself.

"Jerry?" Carol persisted.

Finally she met her eyes.

"Nick," she admitted. "Nick would know all about the materials and how to fake restoration."

Carol's expression was serious. Once again they had left the safety of playful conjecture, and the facts were converging towards something more threatening.

"But, for that matter," continued Jerry hurriedly, "so would Professor Johnson. He has even more experience than Nick, and he would know even more about the restoration side."

They sat in silence, reflecting, sifting, trying to feel where all the bits coalesced into meaning. Jerry abruptly uncurled herself from her chair and stood, trying to shake off the dark mood that had descended over them. "Carol, this is ridiculous, we are only considering the English-speaking restoration world. There are many equally expert restorers and researchers all over Europe. It could have been any one of them."

Carol stood up, too, and gave her a quick hug. "You're completely right," she agreed. "How about a tour around the lake?"

❧

Both of them had grown up spending long hot summers in the cottage district north of Toronto. As children, each had spent at least a month every year at camps where they had been trained to manage all kinds of boats. Besides a rowboat there was a large fibreglass canoe, which they hauled over to the dock from its resting place on the shore. As Jerry settled into the front, her knees sank into foam pads permanently attached to the bottom of the canoe. "Remember those wooden canoes they had at camp? I never managed to have enough clothing to pad my knees properly. Why didn't they use foam then?"

Carol laughed as she took her place in the back. "Come on, Jerry, that was probably before foam was invented."

"No way," she answered, as she took a long pull in the water with her paddle, her arms finding the form naturally as though she did this every day. "It was probably a conscious decision to deny us the comfort of foam, too cushy for wilderness training. We might have gone soft!"

They guided the canoe through a narrow opening into the adjacent bay. As they glided forward, they automatically took care not to bang the sides of the canoe with their paddles and to proceed as quietly as possible. But it was the wrong time to see any wildlife except for birds. To catch sight of the beaver or deer that inhabited the area, they'd have to get up very early in the morning, or take the canoe out just before dusk.

When they'd explored this same bay the evening before, the water had had a totally different quality. Then, it had been still, mirror-like, unruffled by the light breezes that sprang up during the day. They had heard the sharp slap of a beaver's tail on the water as he warned the others of their presence. Just after, they saw a beaver swimming out towards the centre of the bay, trying to lead them away from the lodge, which no doubt contained their young. Now in the hot afternoon, the air buzzed with insects, and birds carried on long involved conversations in the trees. Jerry and Carol made a quick tour of the bay more for the exercise than the view. They turned back out into the main lake, where they continued their journey, hugging the shoreline. Carol wanted to show her the beaver dam just built that spring.

"It's huge," said Jerry softly, as they rocked gently in the canoe, looking at the freshly built dam. "What will you do? Can you get someone to dismantle it?"

"No. I won't bother. For one thing, they'll only build it back up again. They're pretty determined. One of the cottagers in the lake next to ours had an ongoing battle with the beavers all last summer. Every time he took their dam apart, they rebuilt it — overnight."

"But what about the water level? You said it's getting low, won't that be a problem?"

"Not really. The only worry is for swimming off the dock. Now that the water's so low, the rocks are much closer to the surface. It's way too shallow to dive there now. We just have to be careful to remember that."

They continued around the lakeshore until they were back at the cottage. By then the day was truly hot and they finished with a refreshing swim.

Later that evening, sitting around after dinner, they returned to the subject they had left earlier. "If Nick did all the faking himself, then that doesn't fit with Nick trying to convince me it's a fake, and arranging to have himself kidnapped," said Jerry from her easy chair.

"You're right. Nick the faker would want to get the thing sold as soon as possible. It certainly wouldn't be in his interest to try and convince you it was a fake. But he might blow up your loft to shut you up," added Carol helpfully.

"Thanks, Carol," retorted Jerry dryly. "Since the facts we have don't fit with Nick being responsible for faking the painting, then maybe we can drop that theory."

"Okay. Now, what about the owner? Is there an owner *and* a faker, or are they one and the same?" asked Carol.

"Good question, but does it matter?"

"You know, Andrew could actually be as innocent as he sounded. The owner-faker could have blown up your loft; Andrew didn't have to have anything to do with it."

Jerry agreed. If Andrew had passed on to the owner their conversation about Jerry getting medium analysis done, the owner could have acted alone. If Andrew were innocent, then maybe he would help them find out who faked the painting, she mused aloud.

"Really, Jerry," replied Carol. "If you just received I-don't-know-how-many millions of dollars for your share in the sale of a Vermeer, would you turn around and help someone discover if it was a fake? Please!"

Carol was right. It was highly unlikely that Andrew would be very forthcoming — knowingly, that is.

On Sunday as Jerry helped tidy the cottage and load up the car for their return journey, she felt light-hearted and happy. In their many conversations about the events surrounding the sale of the painting, they had not managed to build a very convincing case against Nick, either as someone attempting to drive the price down or as the person behind its elaborate fabrication. While she was willing to accept Andrew's protestations of innocence, Nick's involvement still wasn't logical; the owner could just as easily be suspected. That felt much better. She had not wanted to admit to herself how troubled she was by her doubts about Nick.

Jerry and Carol arrived in Toronto late Sunday afternoon. The cats had slept the whole way back in the car, but as soon as Carol turned onto her street, Alvin and Tony were awake instantly and lept to the car windows meowing.

"How do they know it's their street?" asked Carol, trying to control the car and simultaneously swat at Tony who had jumped onto her lap to look out of her side window. Alvin, in his excitement, was trying to look everywhere at once, which meant rushing from window to window, including the one Tony was using. Carol ended up with both of them on her lap, each struggling for the best view. Jerry was quietly trying to disentangle Alvin from the mess of cat fur and limbs, while murmuring her apologies. Carol, thoroughly fed up, shouted, "Enough!" This had an immediate effect on both cats, who promptly used her lap as a launching pad, digging their claws in for purchase as they made their collective escape.

Jerry looked on guiltily, watching Carol's grimace as she silently weathered cat claws digging into her skin. One of these days she's going to get fed up with her and her damn cats, thought Jerry miserably. Carol enjoyed Alvin and Tony when they were behaving themselves, but she didn't have the natural empathy of a committed cat owner. Jerry was hardly in a position to admonish her for shouting at them, but she knew that if Carol had just spoken calmly, none of the panicked claw-digging would have happened.

By the time they had pulled into the underground parking lot and were unloading the car, the heavy silence hanging over them was lifting. Jerry caught Carol's eye and when she smiled back, gave her a quick hug. "You're awfully good to us," said Jerry shyly. "I wouldn't know what to do without you."

Carol reassured her, "Don't worry, Jerry. I don't quite have the hang of those two yet. I know they didn't mean any harm."

Both cats, sensing the tense atmosphere in the car, had become extremely subdued. They got into their carriers obediently in preparation for the trip up to the apartment.

The message light on the phone was flashing when they got in. It was Nick asking Jerry to call him so they could arrange their holiday together. Jerry was caught between excitement and remorse. She was eager to see Nick, but she worried about imposing on Carol by leaving her with the cats again, especially after what had just happened in the car. She wandered into the kitchen to find Carol fixing a hot drink and giving the cats their dinner.

"Was that Nick?" Carol asked as she poured boiling water into the teapot. Jerry, getting out the cups and saucers, murmured yes.

"You don't sound very happy."

"He wants me to fly over and have a holiday with him."

"That sounds great, Jerry. Why aren't you crazed with delight? Still worrying about whether he's somehow involved in the painting scam?"

"No," she answered, then hesitated. "I just feel bad about always leaving you with the cats."

"Oh, for heaven's sake, that's ridiculous. I'm perfectly happy to have them. They're really no trouble. And anyway, I rather like their company." As Carol finished her sentence, Tony, never one to be demonstrative, walked over and rubbed against her leg, giving one of Carol's bare toes a quick raspy lick. Jerry shook her head as she watched Carol bend over to give him a grateful pat — what a sense of timing he had. Who said they were dumb animals?

❧

The night before she was due to leave, Jerry was relaxing with a good book in the living room. Carol sat down across from her.

"Jerry," she started hesitantly, "I want to talk to you about Nick before you go."

"Okay, what about him?" she answered warily.

"How well do you know this guy? Have you ever met any of his friends? What about his family, his parents? You told me he's divorced. Do you know what happened?"

Jerry felt her heart sinking — not the Nick thing again. The trouble was, Carol had a point. She didn't know that much about him. There had never been an opportunity for her to meet any of his friends or to see him in any "normal" context. When they met in Cambridge, there was no one else around. They were alone that weekend in Ottawa, and the next time was in Nice and Italy when everything was so tense. She knew Carol was right, but it still made her feel defensive. She couldn't help herself, she responded testily. "*That* is what this visit is all about, Carol."

"Come on, Jerry. Don't get upset. We really should talk about this."

"He emails me all the time. It's true he doesn't talk about himself much, but he's ... I don't know how to explain it ... he's kind, considerate ... he seems to be such a good person."

Carol sighed, "I don't think you can go by that. Appearances can be deceiving, especially on email. There are so many stories about people ..."

"Carol! Stop it! I know what he's like. I can feel it!" Jerry insisted.

"You can't be sure, especially about feelings. Look at the effects psychopaths can have on people."

"What are you talking about!" Jerry burst out, furious. "Now you're saying he's a psychopath!?"

"Calm down. I was only trying to give you an example. I've been reading this really interesting book about psychopaths. They can totally fool people into thinking they're perfectly normal. They're very smooth operators. Even doctors who study them can get taken in."

Jerry rolled her eyes at Carol and shook her head. "So that's what this is about. Every time you read a new book, it's like the flavour of the month. You get a new piece of information and try to make it apply to everything." She stood up, on the verge of leaving the room.

"I don't think you're being fair. I'm worried about you. There's something really dangerous going on. Somebody tried to kill you, and we still don't know who it was."

"Carol. We know it was someone who wanted to shut me up about the Vermeer. Now that it's sold, there's nothing I can do, so there's no more reason for me to be in danger. We have to be logical."

"That's just it, Jerry. It may be logical to us, but not necessarily to whoever set this up. They could still see you as a threat.

They may just be waiting for the right opportunity. And you still don't know where Nick fits in."

"Nick is on my side."

"You don't know that for sure. Remember, psychopaths lie, and they lie very convincingly. You have to be careful."

"You and your psychopaths. Honestly, Carol. I know you mean well but ..." Jerry bit back the rest of her sentence. She took a deep breath, and finished, "I'll be careful. You're right. I shouldn't be too trusting."

The conversation thoroughly rattled Jerry. She had to admit that there was a lot about Nick she still didn't know, and it was unsettling to think that whoever had been willing to kill her was still out there somewhere. She had trouble sleeping that night. Her restlessness eventually drove Alvin and Tony off the bed; they jumped down in disgust and went looking for a quieter place to sleep.

❧

Jerry arrived in London a few days before she and Nick were due to go off on their holiday together. One of the people she wanted to see was Ben Johnson at the Chelsea Institute of Art. She arrived early for their meeting and was shown up to the studio by one of the senior students. Three of them were bent over their easels in front of the bank of windows, the last to finish off their paintings before the summer break. Jerry stopped to talk with each of them in turn. All three were in the final stages of their treatments, inpainting areas of lost paint to reintegrate the images. It was a nice bright day, the light was good, and the students were making the most of it. Jerry was admiring the high quality of their work when Professor Johnson came to get her.

He introduced Jerry to the students with a mock flourish. "Of course you all realize that this is the famous Ms. McPherson who found the Vermeer." They immediately peppered her with excited questions. Overwhelmed, she laughed and tried her best to answer, carefully omitting the part about its being a fake. Professor Johnson eventually rescued her and led her away to his office. She found it as cluttered as ever, but took note of the painting on his easel waiting for final touches before varnishing. It was a small but very engaging oil-sketch by Tiepolo, the pastel shades of pink and blue a delightful confection. He caught her eye. "Lovely, isn't it? One of the perks of our profession. I get to have it all to myself for a while."

Knowing that he would likely be eager to hear about her work on the Vermeer, Jerry had brought a set of photographs. He was particularly interested in the removal of the painting that had been on top. He questioned her closely on how easy it was to get rid of the residue; was it possible to clean the Vermeer completely? She assured him that it was and that the paint had been in perfect condition after cleaning. They talked about the evidence, which showed that the materials were all consistent with Vermeer's time. When Jerry started to talk about the discovery of the resin in the paint, and Nick's find that it was anachronistic, he interrupted her. "Jerry, you must put all of the unfortunate aspects of this case behind you. It won't do to dwell on them." He continued, "I was so sorry to hear that your studio was destroyed, you must be feeling terribly dispossessed. But now you and Nick have started something very positive between you, and you'll be at the South Kensington. You must get a fresh start. Look to the future, my dear."

Jerry was taken aback by his sudden, uncharacteristic foray into fatherly advice, but she thanked him for his concern and explained that she was resigned to the fact that nothing would be gained by further investigation. She tried to bring the subject back to the Vermeer, she wanted his opinion on the resin that had been identified. But he suddenly looked at his watch, stood up and declared he had forgotten an important meeting.

Since this was the way meetings with Professor Johnson usually ended, Jerry was not particularly put out as she watched him disappear down the stairs calling goodbye and clutching a bunch of loose papers to his chest. She was used to his eccentricities by now. However she was disappointed that the discussion about the kauri copal in Vermeer's paint had been interrupted. Andrew had been adamant that no one could identify the actual type of copal resin in an old paint sample. Since he had questioned Nick's information, she had been looking forward to hearing Professor Johnson's opinion, and to be reassured that Andrew had it wrong — not Nick.

Between lunching with friends and attending dinner parties, the next few days passed quickly. She visited her old haunts and had a nostalgic afternoon in Hampstead, refreshing her memory of that wonderful part of London where she had lived when she was an intern at the Chelsea. Her wanderings took her down Church Row to the small churchyard at the bottom of the street. She made a respectful visit to Constable's grave, delighting in the overgrown and generally unkempt condition of the graveyard, which added so much to its ancient atmosphere.

Despite her pleasure in rediscovering London, thoughts of Nick were never very far. Yet her feelings were mixed. She anxiously tried to picture the moment she would get off the train in Cambridge where he would be waiting for her. Would he sense her unease? She still felt the weight of that last conversation with Carol. Her parting shot about psychopaths being such good liars had unnerved Jerry. How could she know she could trust him? She wished she had taken a look at Carol's book so she could see for herself. Psychopaths! How ridiculous! Nick couldn't possibly be lying to her, she would know. Wouldn't she?

Chapter 21

IT WAS A BEAUTIFUL SUNNY DAY. Jerry's train arrived around noon to find Nick waiting for her on the platform. They gave each other an exuberant hug. All thoughts of Andrew's accusations and Carol's worries flew away the moment she saw him. As they turned towards the exit, she averted her face, embarrassed by the tears that had suddenly come from nowhere. He brushed her wet cheek and softly murmured, "What is this?"

"Nothing. Just ... just glad to see you," she said, flustered.

He answered with a fierce hug. She was still trying to catch her breath when they arrived at the car. As she got in, she noticed a picnic hamper in the backseat. "Are we eating on the road? How long will we be driving?" she asked as he settled into the driver's seat and put the car in gear.

"It'll take about five hours. I thought we might stop somewhere along the way and eat outside, it's such a marvellous day."

"When will you tell me where we're going? All I know is that we are vacationing somewhere in England."

"You'll see."

"At least tell me the direction. East, west, north, south?"

"North."

As green fields sped by the window, Jerry chatted comfortably with Nick, filling him in on her activities in London.

"How was your meeting with Ben?" he asked.

Jerry shrugged happily. "The usual. We were just getting to something interesting when he had to rush off."

Nick laughed. "Typical. But you'll have a chance to see him again. I've invited him for dinner when we're back in Cambridge next week."

"That'll be nice," Jerry responded carefully. She was remembering the oddly personal conversation he had with her about getting over the Vermeer and settling down, presumably with Nick. She hoped he wouldn't embarrass her by bringing up the subject again in front of him. The bright sunlight and beautiful scenery outside the car soon captured her attention and she stopped worrying. She decided she might as well take the professor's advice. To hell with the Vermeer and Andrew and everything, she was just going to enjoy herself. The last time she and Nick had been together and worry-free was in Ottawa in the spring. She was determined that this would be an extension of that weekend.

Most of their journey took place on the motorway, so Jerry's exposure to the countryside was in tantalizing glimpses. Eventually, they left the crush of constant traffic and took off across country along small laneways bordered by ancient hedges. Nick drove along the narrow roads at what felt to Jerry like breakneck speed; she wasn't used to hurtling along and worrying that they might meet another car at every upcoming bend. Just when she was wishing they were back on the motorway, they rounded another corner and she let out a gasp of surprise.

"Castle Howard! I didn't know it was around here!" she cried out, delighted to be confronted by the historic house. Nick pulled into the parking lot. As they emerged from the air-conditioned car, they were met with a blast of hot humid air. She'd forgotten how close it could get in the summer heat in England.

"I thought you might enjoy having a look around. It'll be a nice break from the car. We'll see the house, then we can wander the grounds a bit. I know a spot where we can picnic just up the road."

As they approached the huge stately home, loud, almost eerie, cries pierced the still air. Jerry turned in the direction of the sound to find two peacocks strutting about with their tails on full display. They enjoyed watching their haughty demeanor for a while, then Nick took her hand and they went inside for the house tour. It was a relief to be indoors. It would be weeks before hot weather penetrated these cavernous interiors. They explored the cool rooms with pleasure.

Later, not far from the estate, they found a patch of shade under an ancient oak tree. Nick pulled out a linen tablecloth and matching serviettes from the picnic hamper and spread the cloth out over the rough grass. Over the fresh cool linen he piled dishes and bowls. As he uncorked a bottle of rosé, she arranged cold chicken, potato salad, and a loaf of crusty bread in front of them. The food was delicious; the rosé dry and cold.

Insects buzzed lazily in the air. The combination of full stomachs, heat, and wine caught up with them. Nick leaned against the tree with Jerry in his arms. She nestled on his chest and both fell deeply asleep.

They woke with a start hours later when the first drops of rain hit the ground. Quickly gathering their picnic, they raced to the car, reaching it just as the clouds opened in earnest. They drove on with the windscreen wipers fighting the rain, the daylight now a dusky blue.

"Do we still have a long way to go?" she asked.

"No. Just under an hour. Sorry I fell asleep, I only meant to nap. I had wanted you to see the moors as we cross them and to be there in time for you to have a good look around before dinner. Now with this rain, it's all going to be dark," he said, disappointed.

"I've been enjoying every minute so far, even the rain," she said brightly. "The moors! I've never seen them."

"Well you won't tonight, either," he said brusquely, still put out by their long sleep.

He was right. It was impossible to see anything out the window while they crossed the moors. Eventually the rain let up and in the deep blue of the evening light she was just able to make out deep valleys and hills in the countryside ahead. "How beautiful!" she breathed with her nose almost pressed up against the glass. "Where are we?"

"Just outside Whitby. It's a fishing town where my parents keep a holiday home. I thought you would enjoy being up in Yorkshire. You'll find it quite different from London," replied Nick, shifting the car into low gear. They were heading down a very steep incline as they dipped into one of the deeper valleys.

By the time Nick had pulled the car into a spot on the street outside his parents' home, the rain had stopped altogether. They stepped out onto dark streets slick with wet. The reflections of a series of small white lights strung up along the harbour shone back off the asphalt as they gathered their things from the car. Jerry felt tired from the day's journey, but the salty sea air was cool and refreshing.

She followed Nick through a narrow passageway between the rows of houses facing the harbour, and found herself climbing wet stone stairs. Nick called out, "Be careful these steps are slippery." She caught herself in time, shifted her assortment of baggage, and started up again more carefully. It was very dark. Just as they started to lose the light that penetrated the passageway from the street, the stairway was suddenly illuminated by powerful lights, triggered by their presence. Now she could see the substantial climb ahead of her — the steps went on forever! Finally, feeling thoroughly out of shape, she reached the top, facing a huge old house. It was perched on the side of the hill, looking out over Whitby harbour.

Nick inserted a huge wrought-iron key in the door. The lock turned with a single thunk and the door swung noiselessly inwards. The air in the hallway smelled slightly damp and musty, the odour of a house that had been shut up for some time. But the chill atmosphere of neglect was soon dispelled as Nick moved from room to room switching on lights, and Jerry could see a comfortable home unfolding before her.

She followed him through spacious rooms furnished by well-chosen antiques. It was nothing like the tiny cottage she had pictured when Nick said his parents kept a "holiday home." He lit a fire in the upstairs living room then opened a small cupboard beside the fireplace and switched on the central heating. He rubbed his arms and then Jerry's. "It'll soon warm up," he said, smiling down at her. Her heart skipped a beat when she saw his smile. He really is extraordinarily attractive, she thought, feeling suddenly shy and awkward.

Neither of them was particularly hungry after their elaborate lunch, and both agreed they were too tired to enjoy dinner in a restaurant that evening. Instead they finished unpacking the car, then grazed on what was left from their picnic. Jerry was looking forward to an early night and to going to bed — with Nick.

The next morning, they woke to a strong sun, which easily

penetrated the antique lace curtains by their bed. Jerry was in no hurry to get up, and neither, it seemed was Nick. He reached over to her and they continued last night's languorous love-making. Just what this holiday together was supposed to be about, she thought with satisfaction afterwards as she lay in bed while Nick dozed beside her. None of the tension of our last time together.

Involuntarily, she began picturing the Hotel Negresco and Nick sitting on the edge of the bed, talking into the phone. Then Carol, questioning whether it was a set-up: was he really talking to the police? She screwed her eyes shut and pulled a pillow over her head, willing herself not to think about it.

It was no use, once the anxiety had started it was impossible for her to lie still. She softly crept out of the room and downstairs to the kitchen. She was standing in her nightgown, absently staring out at some seagulls on the roof of the house below them, when Nick found her. "What are you doing?" he asked, as he stood behind her and put his arms around her shoulders.

"Nothing. Just enjoying the view."

"No you weren't. Something's troubling you." He turned her around. "Jerry look at me. What is it? The painting?"

She nodded and tried to move away. But he held her there, and gave her a little shake. "You can't let it ruin things. We'll probably never know for sure who was behind it."

"I know. It's just that ..." She couldn't finish. Just that what? Just that I can never trust you because there will always be some suspicion? She couldn't say that to him. Anyway, it was a theoretical issue, her feelings were very clear, it was only her brain that got in the way. She gave him a hug, and smiled. "You're right, Nick. I'm going to forget all about it. Right now!" she pushed him towards the kitchen door. "We're going to get dressed and go out for a walk."

Once back down the steps and through the passageway between the houses, they turned towards the old part of the town. The air was fresh, the sun warm, and white clouds dotted a blue sky. Jerry had heard of Whitby, famous for its association with Captain Cook, the eighteenth-century explorer, and for the hauntingly beautiful ruins of Whitby Abbey where Bram Stoker had set the scene for the arrival in England of Count Dracula. The town lay along both sides of a deep estuary that formed a natural harbour. It was a pleasure to explore on foot. They walked leisurely through narrow cobble-stoned streets taking in the mixture of holiday shops selling sweets, pastries, and nicknacks and shops for the locals selling fresh produce, clothing, and — most compelling of all since they were nearing lunchtime — fresh fish. Jerry stopped in front of the large picture window of a fish shop, eyeing the stuffed crab with evident longing. Nick tugged on her arm. "Not here, I know another shop. Come on, it's the one we always go to."

They walked farther up the street, then turned right, passing through a small square with an ancient-looking covered market. There, people were selling a variety of cheap and cheerful household goods. Jerry slowed to have a better look, but Nick took her hand and led her on, heading left into the main street that wound towards the sea. As they continued down the cobblestones, the street narrowed and looked like it would end in a cul-de-sac, but then it suddenly opened out, and they were at the foot of the steps leading up to the Abbey. To the right of the steps the street narrowed into extinction. Nick headed down to the end, and there, tucked almost under the steps, was a fish store.

They picked out two large stuffed crabs and some fresh-cooked shrimp. The fishmonger wrapped their purchases in plain newsprint paper before placing them in a plastic bag. Jerry was surprised at the cost; it was so much less than in London. Next Nick took her down a small street to the left of the stairs, where there was a shop selling smoked kippers. The wonderful smell of wood smoke permeated everything inside because the smoke house was right next door.

On their way back, as they passed the great series of stone steps leading up to the Abbey, Jerry hesitated, but Nick gave her another little tug. "We'll come back and do the Abbey properly. Now let's get back for lunch, I'm starving."

She happily fell into step alongside him. They made a final stop at a small fish and chip shop where Nick bought them a double order of chips to go with their crab and shrimp. Back in the house they ate with relish, washing it down with a cold bottle of Chablis that Nick had brought along from Cambridge. Their lunch reduced to debris on the table, they sat in companionable silence finishing the wine. A smile passed between the two of them. Light-headed and feeling the wine, she stood up slowly, but only managed to get as far as Nick's lap. She wound her arms around his neck and gave him an affectionate kiss. He laughed and stood up, holding her in his arms as though she weighed nothing at all. He swung her around and put her down; by now she was laughing as well. They made their way up the stairs and flopped on the bed together, still laughing, caught up in the sheer pleasure of being together.

That afternoon, they walked up the hundred-and-ninety-nine steps to St. Mary's Church at the foot of the Abbey. Jerry was fascinated; she had never been inside a church like it. The floor was a maze of family booths consisting of boxed pews that functioned as a series of separate rooms, their sides shoulder high. Inside each, wooden benches lined the walls. She sat in one, trying to imagine what it would have been like a hundred years ago. She pictured the minister preaching from his three-tiered pulpit to families crammed into the booths; each group separated from their neighbours by the wooden walls. Even in June the air inside was cold and damp. "It must have been freezing in here in the winter," she said. "All the better to be tucked in together as close as possible."

They toured the Abbey afterwards, but Jerry found it disappointing. The building looked much more interesting and commanding from afar. She preferred to see it towering at the top of the hill looking out over Whitby and the sea, rather than up close where it was reduced to a pile of stones, the ruined walls an echo of what it must have been.

In the evening, they dressed warmly against the damp, sharp air and walked to a local restaurant where Nick assured her she would have the best and biggest portion of fish and chips in the North. Despite her small size, Jerry had an enormous appetite. She had no trouble keeping up with Nick as they each devoured the contents of a large plate heaped with crispy battered fish and hot chips — brown on the outside but firm and white inside. The cool night air was refreshing as they sauntered back to the house feeling happy and sleepy.

The days passed in much the same way. Jerry felt herself unwinding and developing a deep contentment as she savoured the pleasure of Nick's company in this lovely setting. She couldn't remember being happier. Carol's warnings seemed absurd.

In the second week, on their last day in Whitby, Nick took her to the local museum on the other side of the harbour. Nothing in the rather austere entrance of the museum with its two galleries on either side devoted to paintings and watercolours prepared her for what was to come. She spent some time in the gallery on the left, looking at the Weatherills, beautiful Turneresque seascapes, so skillfully rendered she found herself responding with delight. Unlike Turner, whose paintings tend to disappear into an indistinct swirl of colour and mist the closer one gets to the surface, these paintings were executed with minute attention to detail. Along one wall were a series of his watercolour drawings; his draughtsmanship was outstanding. She could have inspected the delicate drawings and colours all day. Nick, who had wandered into the other gallery across the hall, returned to find her locked in place in front of the watercolours. He stood and watched for some time, taking in her graceful shape, her dark shining hair and small exquisite features. She gradually became aware of his presence and dragged herself away from the paintings. She turned to look at him, startled by the serious expression on his face.

"Nick, is there something wrong? What's bothering you?" she asked softly.

"Nothing," he answered quickly. "Come and see the rest of the museum."

"You mean there's more?" She followed him eagerly back to the central hallway and realized that she had been so caught up in looking at the paintings, she hadn't noticed the door leading to the rest of the museum. They paid the entrance fee, and found themselves transported back at least a hundred years to the most wonderful assortment of curiosities ever collected by the Victorians. Cabinet after cabinet stood in rows, their wavy glass fronts housing countless items from previous centuries. Jerry was enchanted. It was such a treat to find a museum that had not had its displays vandalized by twentieth-century modernization, the original display cabinets replaced by plexiglass, the number of objects reduced to a bare minimum.

Whereas she found modern exhibitions self-conscious and devoid of atmosphere, here she could recapture a sense of wonder and discovery, as if she were seeing everything through Victorian eyes. Objects were lovingly displayed, just as they had been when originally brought to the museum. Cards, handwritten in copper-point, described whatever the owners could relate about their gifts. Jerry found her favourite section quickly: the domestic life of the inhabitants of Whitby — old eyeglasses, snuff boxes, and a selection of fire-starting implements from flint to the first match-es. The treasures were laid out in dusty profusion. In one case was a mummified human hand; the card explained that this was a thief's lucky charm, to be carried for protection while on the job. Jerry was utterly entranced. Nick, too, enjoyed the visit because he was sharing one of his favourite places with her. He pointed out cabinets full of objects and displays he had delighted in as a child. They were reluctantly evicted when the museum closed.

They lingered in the park outside the museum, sitting on a wooden bench from which they could survey the harbour. From their vantage point, high on one side looking out over the River Esk, they could see across to Nick's parents' eighteenth-century house on the opposite hill. They were the only ones left in the park. Nick caressed Jerry's hand absently, his eyes on the scene in front of them.

"Jerry. This week with you here has confirmed something I think I've known ever since the day I met you. I can't imagine my life without you in it."

Jerry felt her stomach tingling with butterflies as he spoke. She knew she had been falling in love for months, but hearing it from Nick was wonderful and terrifying at the same time. She felt weak with emotion. She couldn't speak; she squeezed his hand in response.

"When I came in to the gallery and watched you looking at those watercolours, it all hit me, and I realized how close I came to losing you in that loft explosion. I want us to be together," he said quietly.

Jerry finally found the courage to look at him. She smiled

shyly and nodded. She felt she should really try to snap out of this swoon she was in; it was getting ridiculous.

"When my papers come through, I'll be able to move here ...," she said, her voice sounding small and wavery. She frowned at herself, what had happened to her voice?

"But you'll be in London. My work is in Cambridge. I know some people commute, but I don't want that. I want us to be living in the same house," he smiled, "and sharing the same bed. *Every night,* not just on weekends."

She turned her face towards him. Her eyes were wide, her expression completely vulnerable. He kissed her lightly. She kissed him with feeling. It was easier to express herself that way than in words.

"But my job ... I'll have to live in London ...," she started.

"We could set up a studio for you in Cambridge, you could do private work," he interrupted.

"But if I don't take the job in London, then I won't have the papers I need to live in England."

"We could get married." There, he'd said it. The words were finally out.

They sat in silence. Jerry's feelings turned to dread. Carol's warnings came rushing back. All her instincts were urging her to accept, but she didn't know what to do, it was all happening too fast. Jerry was looking down at their hands, still entwined. "I would like that," she said simply; she was about to say, "but ..." when he responded.

"So would I."

She let out the long breath she had been unconsciously holding. She felt a surge of relief and exhilaration followed rapidly by a crushing weight. This was supposed to be a wonderful moment, yet it was so mixed up in her mind. She turned to him, wanting to explain, to buy time, but when she saw his face, she couldn't help it. She just shook her head and smiled, no, radiated with pure pleasure. To hell with it, she thought. I'll worry about this later.

Chapter 22

NICK HAD PLANNED THAT THEY WOULD ALSO GO up to Scotland for a brief tour. But now he was eager for Jerry to meet his parents. They lived in a village in the Cotswolds near Gloucester. With only a few days left in their vacation, he suggested they forgo their trip to Scotland and visit them for a night on their way back to Cambridge. Jerry's heart sank. Meeting his parents as the "prospective bride" was the last thing she wanted to do. But she knew if she raised any objections, she would have to confess her misgivings to Nick, and it would open a chasm between them. He seemed so happy, she could not bear to bring it up yet. Anyway, what was she going to say?

Jerry pictured the conversation: "Um, Nick. I'm not sure I can marry you after all."

"Why?"

"Carol thinks you might be a psychopath: you could have been lying to me all along about the Vermeer."

She sighed bitterly. While she was at it, she might as well throw in: "And by the way, Nick, I'm not so sure I want to give up the job in London for the expense of setting up a private studio in Cambridge."

So Jerry decided the best action was none at all. She would go along with what her heart felt was perfectly natural, and try to curb the uneasiness in her mind. Meanwhile, she was going to feel like a complete imposter when Nick announced their plans to his parents.

For the first night of their trip south, after leaving Whitby, Nick had again kept their destination a surprise. They had left Whitby after lunch, and three hours later Nick was pulling into the parking lot of another large historic house. Privately she was a little dismayed; she had been looking forward to getting to their hotel early. She wasn't really in the mood for another historic house tour.

To her amazement, Nick started unloading their bags from the trunk. She stood staring at him as if he had suddenly gone mad. "Nick! What are you doing?"

"Getting our bags," he answered, with a twinkle in his eyes.

"Why?"

"Because this is where we're staying tonight."

She wheeled around and looked again at the old mansion in front of her. The garden was glorious, flowers were tumbling all over themselves in an excess of colour, late afternoon sunlight was streaming across the lawn. Surely they couldn't afford to stay here!

He led her up the path towards the reception. They entered a large hall with linen-covered sofas and outsized flowers in huge glass vases; Jerry took in the signs of luxury and felt utterly at sea. What was happening? How could Nick want them to stay in such an expensive place? For a moment she allowed herself to take guilty pleasure in their tasteful surroundings. "But ... surely he can't afford this?" she murmured under her breath. This was no longer extenuating circumstances where they needed a Hotel Negresco.

Nick checked them in and came back, key in hand, with a inscrutable expression on his face. "Shall we have a look at our room?"

It was breathtaking. The ceilings were very high, the windows large and surrounded on either side by yards of fabulously rich cloth. The same fabric had been used for the bedspread on the antique four-poster, which was piled with pillows. The bathroom, almost as large as their room, was done entirely in marble. The bath, a jacuzzi, shone brightly back at her, inviting a long soak.

Jerry sank into the feather cushion of a richly upholstered armchair and felt the cool touch of linen. She looked at Nick accusingly. "All right, Nick. What's going on? How can we afford to be here?" she asked quietly.

He smiled uncomfortably. "Actually, Jerry, I thought you might have guessed already," he said. "My family is quite comfortably off. We don't throw it around of course, but, well ...

this is one of my parent's favourite hotels in the area and I thought you would enjoy it." He hesitated. "You seem upset. Are you?"

Now it was Jerry who felt foolish. It had never occurred to her that Nick could be from a wealthy family. She had never paid much attention to details that now seemed blindingly obvious: the smart car, his spacious flat in Cambridge, the beautiful antiques in his parents' house in Whitby.

"Oh," she said quietly, kicking herself. "The room is gorgeous, Nick. Thank you for bringing me here."

He held out his hand, "Let's go and see the garden. You'll love it." She was grateful to him for the ease with which he covered the awkward moment. A tour of the garden would do fine, anything to change the subject.

Later that evening, as they dined in the hotel's restaurant, Jerry could hear Carol whispering in her ear, "How come he's so rich, Jerry? Where did the money come from? Maybe it's not only his parents, maybe he makes millions selling fakes." Jerry looked quickly over at Nick. Her thoughts were crashing around so loudly in her head, for a second she was afraid he had heard what she was thinking. She took a deep breath. She would have to talk to him about the Vermeer. She couldn't avoid it. She needed to go over it all again with him, to reassure herself that he could not possibly have been involved. There was never going to be a good time to bring it up, so she plunged in.

"It just doesn't feel finished," she ventured. "I'm sorry to bring it up. I know you want me to forget about it, but I can't. I can't stop thinking about the forgery — the deception."

"I understand, Jerry, it's hard to forget about it. Especially with the knowledge that whoever set this up has gotten away with it. I don't care so much about the art fraud. Unfortunately it's all too common; one more fake hanging in a gallery really doesn't amount to much in my opinion. But the attempt on your life is something else. I'd like to get to the bottom of that."

"Detective-Sergeant Wiens thinks I ... I mean ... we aren't in any more danger now that the painting has been sold."

"I'm sure he's right," said Nick confidently. "But it galls me to think that someone should get away with attempted murder."

"What about Oscar who found the kauri copal in the Vermeer?

Did he learn anything more about the break-in at his lab?"

"Not much. Oscar never even associated the break-in with the paint sample because other things were missing as well."

"Do *you* think it was related?"

Nick sighed and toyed with his glass. "I don't know what to think. It certainly looked very suspicious at the time. Now I'm not so sure. Maybe it was a coincidence that someone broke in then. It wasn't the first time they've had things stolen, the lab is associated with the university. Usually it's computers or cash."

"It's unnerving to think that whoever is behind the Vermeer fraud had a long-enough reach to stage a break-in at a lab in Amsterdam while simultaneously arranging your kidnapping in Nice."

"Yes. It makes me wonder how many people were involved."

"Or how well organized one person can be," replied Jerry.

The head waiter appeared accompanied by two servers bearing the next course, in covered silver dishes. They placed the dishes in front of Jerry and Nick, then, with a flourish, uncovered their meals at the same moment. Jerry found it all a bit theatrical, but the magret de canard in front of her looked delicious. It was a welcome interruption. She really didn't want to pursue any more questions about the Vermeer. Maybe she could get Carol to shut up long enough for her to enjoy the meal.

Chapter 23

THE NEXT MORNING, THEY WERE UP EARLY. They still had a long drive before they would be in Gloucestershire. As they drove, Jerry's thoughts turned to the evening ahead. Although looking forward to meeting Nick's parents, she was nervous that she might not meet their expectations. Would she be the kind of daughter-in-law they had in mind? Would his mother pick up on her indecision? Nick, on the other hand, appeared to have no doubts. He seemed completely relaxed and unconcerned.

"Are you planning to tell your parents about us tonight?" asked Jerry, feigning a nonchalance she didn't feel.

"Of course," Nick answered. He hesitated, then asked, "Weren't you expecting me to?"

Jerry fidgeted in the car seat, not sure what to say.

"Listen, Jerry, I'm very sure about this. It's what I want. But if you're having second thoughts ..." he trailed off.

"Oh, no!" she lied. "It's just ...," she searched for the words, "it's just that I thought you might want to break it to them slowly. You know, have them meet me first, then, well, tell them our plans a bit later ..."

Nick laughed, and reached over to squeeze her hand. "Don't worry, Jerry. They're going to be thrilled. With you and with our engagement."

Jerry hoped he was right. She was feeling completely inadequate. What if they were expecting someone from the right school, the right family? What about her own misgivings? She should never have agreed to the engagement, she should have insisted they wait. But for what? How would more time solve anything?

She kept finding excuses to stop along the way. She insisted on shopping in a beautiful market town they passed, then found a spot by a river that was "irresistible." Nick was indulgent, and she sensed he knew she was stalling. All too soon, they were on the road to Dursely, the town where Nick's parents lived. Nick made a right into a small lane that turned out to be a long drive-way leading to the house. When Jerry saw the stone manor nestled in the woods, surrounded by a modest garden, she let out a sigh of relief. I can handle this; it's not too imposing after all, she thought to herself.

Nick's parents greeted them at the door, along with a large black Labrador who was thankfully polite enough to leave Jerry alone after a cursory sniff. His mother gave her a warm smile and a little hug.

"I feel like I've met you already," she enthused. "Nick has told us so much about you. Do come in. You must be exhausted from your journey."

Nick's father simply nodded and shook her hand. She wasn't sure what to make of him. In their sitting room, Jerry recognized Nick's parents' taste from her visit to their house in Whitby. But this was more luxurious; rich deep wool carpeting and beautiful antique furniture, softly gleaming with the low lustre of hand-rubbed wax. The room was warm and inviting. She sank into the nearest chair, once again feeling the cool texture of linen and the softness of a feather cushion. No wonder they liked the hotel Nick and I stayed in last night, she thought. Nick's father poured drinks, and his mother served hors-d'oeuvres. Jerry nursed a gin and tonic and tried to unwind. By her second, she began to relax, feeling almost giddy with relief.

Dinner went better than she had expected. Nick's father final-ly warmed up enough to talk to Jerry and they all seemed to get along well. After dessert, Nick cleared his throat, smiled at his par-ents and said, "We have something to tell you."

Jerry's mother looked genuinely pleased. "We were hoping you might."

To celebrate the announcement, Nick's father opened a bottle of champagne. When everyone had toasted each other Nick's mother asked Jerry if she wanted to have a tour of the house. Jerry eagerly agreed, sure that Nick's father would want a word with his son, and she was curious to see the house.

It was a good thing Jerry had had so much gin, wine, and champagne, otherwise she would have been thrown back into her earlier attack of nerves. What had appeared to be a modest home nestled in the woods turned out to have countless rooms richly appointed with beautiful furniture and paintings. She swam through the tour feeling extremely relaxed. After they had seen most of the house, Nick's mother led her into a smaller room where one wall was lined with books. A chaise longue sat in the far corner, the soft glow of a standing lamp illuminating its light creamy-yellow upholstry.

"This is my room. I like to retire here during the day to read," explained his mother.

"It's lovely," Jerry murmured as she walked around. She stopped in front of a small oil painting hanging on the wall above the chaise longue. It was like a precious jewel; she could hardly take her eyes off it. As she looked more closely, she found something oddly familiar about it. Aware that she was taking more time with it than was polite, she turned back to Nick's mother.

"This painting is very beautiful," she said, feeling her words were wholly inadequate.

"It's delightful, isn't it?" his mother replied, coming to stand beside Jerry. "It's Nick's. He knows how much I like it, so he leaves it here for me, on long-term loan," she smiled. They admired it together a little longer, then she said, "Shall we join the men?"

Jerry nodded, and they made their way back to the sitting room to find Nick and his father settled in easy chairs around the fireplace talking companionably. Nick's mother suggested that Nick and Jerry were probably tired and wished to be shown to their room. Jerry was grateful; it had been a very long day and she was longing to be alone with Nick.

Chapter 24

JERRY AND NICK WENT DOWN TO BREAKFAST the next morning, with their things packed and ready to go. Nick was im-patient to get back to Cambridge now that they were only about three hours from home. Jerry had had a restless night. She put it down to the excess of wine and champagne and promised herself she would be more careful the next time. She was surprised at how comfortable she still felt with Nick's mother and father at breakfast. They seemed to accept her completely. Her fears about Nick's involvement with the Vermeer felt foolish; she was glad she had trusted her heart. Perhaps the whispering from Carol would be gone now, too.

They arrived in Cambridge just before lunch. They deposited their things in the hallway of Nick's flat, then he went next door to collect Minou who had been staying with his neighbour Joyce. As he arrived back carrying her, Minou stared balefully at Jerry from the security of her master's arms. Jerry decided she would have to find a way to befriend her, and soon.

They walked down to the café where they had had their first dinner together and ate a quick lunch. The next hour was spent buying ingredients for the dinner they would serve that evening to Professor Johnson. "I'm looking forward to seeing him tonight," said Jerry, when they were heading back to the flat, their arms full of groceries.

"I can't remember a time when I haven't known him. Ben was my tutor, you know. Here. Before he went to the Chelsea Institute of Art."

"He was at Cambridge?"

"Yes. After he read classics he decided to pursue art history. But even then he was painting."

"It's hard to imagine him as a younger man. He looks like he has been a benevolent old professor forever."

"He really hasn't changed much. He was always old. You know what I mean? Some people are born looking like they should retire."

Jerry laughed. "I hope he won't suddenly dash off in the middle of dessert tonight. You know how he's always having to rush off to something else."

Nick smiled. "That's our man. He certainly is predictable."

As they walked, Jerry was struggling to remember why the painting she had seen in Nick's mother's study was so familiar. It was probably painted by someone quite well-known. This frequently happened to her — she'd see a work of art in a gallery or a museum that triggered a link to the images she'd seen in her art history courses, but she wouldn't be able to recall the artist. It was infuriating, like having something on the tip of your tongue.

As they unpacked the groceries in the kitchen, Minou hovered around Nick hopefully. Jerry watched her out of the corner of her eye. So, she thought, you're not immune to the dictates of your little cat stomach are you? She got out the portion of chicken livers she had purchased, sautéd them lightly, and put them aside to cool. Minou steadfastly ignored her.

While Jerry and Nick prepared dinner, the chicken livers cooled on the counter. Nick made the vinaigrette and Jerry washed the salad. She glanced over at Minou. Was she beginning to look a little petulant? Timing was everything with cats, she couldn't delay too long. Taking a saucer from the cupboard, she placed a selection of plump chicken livers in the centre, and began cutting them up. Minou, alert to that special sound of potential cat food being chopped finely, hovered with increased intensity. With a silent flourish, Jerry swept the plate off the counter and placed it directly in front of her. Minou couldn't help herself. She could no longer affect disdain, she dove in. Jerry knew their relationship was about to improve.

Professor Johnson arrived promptly. He looked as rumpled as usual, as though he had had to tear himself away at the last minute from something else to attend dinner. They sat in the kitchen sipping at a sharp but refreshing Sancerre chilled for the occasion. Nick was still involved with last-minute preparations for their meal; he chopped garlic and ginger while Professor Johnson inquired about their vacation. They sat down to their meal with the professor still asking pointed questions about their holiday. He finally inveigled it out of them.

"Bravo!!" he cried when they confessed their plans. He excused himself, disappeared out the front door, and returned with a bottle of champagne. "Here, Nick. Put this in the freezer. We'll have it with dessert to celebrate."

Throughout the meal, Jerry stifled a growing sense of unease. She couldn't let go of the image of the painting she had seen the night before. Something about it wasn't right. What was it that was bothering her? It wasn't only that it reminded her of another painting. Whatever was nagging at the edge of her consciousness was disquieting as well. She tried to keep her attention focused on the conversation at the table, but despite herself, she was distracted.

Suddenly, the connection came to her. She froze, her fork halfway to her mouth. It was the foliage. The foliage in the painting last night was the *same* as the foliage in the painting she had removed from the Vermeer. The next realization crept up on her like something crawling up her spine: it was Nick's! His mother had said the painting was Nick's! He'd painted that foliage ... It must have been him! He must have done the painting on top of the Vermeer!

Abruptly and without a word, she pushed back her chair, got up from the table, and went straight out the kitchen door. She stumbled into the dark garden, her mind racing. None of it made sense, but the evidence was inescapable. That painting on top had to be by the same person who set up the fake Vermeer. She sat with a sharp jolt onto a small stone bench in a corner of the backyard. If only he had told me the truth, she thought thickly, no matter how, I could have rationalized it. I could have found a way to excuse him ... but lies ... there's nothing I can do with lies ...

Nick found her on the bench, bent over and shakily stroking Minou, who was rubbing against her ankles in commiseration.

"Jerry! What is it?" he asked, his voice soft and concerned.

"I can't talk to you. Not now," she pleaded.

He sat down beside her. "You must tell me, maybe I can help."

Silence.

"Jerry, please."

In spite of herself, she felt compelled to speak. "I know ... I know about you," she whispered.

"What do you know?" His voice took on an edge of exasperation. "Jerry, what are you talking about?"

"The painting ... it was bothering me ever since I saw it last night. Your painting has the same foliage. I recognized the brushwork. It's the same as the foliage in the painting that was on top of the Vermeer."

"My painting?" he sounded puzzled.

"I saw it at your parents' house last night. I was admiring it in your mother's study and she told me it was yours."

It took a moment for him to realize what she was talking about. "It *is* mine, Jerry. But I didn't paint it!"

"But ... but I thought when she said it was yours ... that you did it."

"No. Ben did. He gave it to me years ago, when I was an undergraduate. My mother always loved it, so I gave it to her."

Jerry felt like someone who had suddenly been thrown clear of a car that was careening out of control. She looked at him. "How stupid of me! Oh, Nick, please forgive me. I don't know how I could have thought for a second that you ..."

He pulled her into his arms and rocked her back and forth.

Just then, they heard the professor calling out to them. They looked up and saw him framed in the door, the light from the kitchen throwing his figure into silhouette.

"I'm sorry to break this up, but I'm afraid I shall have to go," he started. But before he could finish his sentence, the light behind him exploded into a searing white flash, throwing his body forward into the garden. The sound of the explosion was deafening. In one movement they were up and running to his side. He lay crumpled, his arms and legs all wrong. Jerry knelt beside him among the glass, bricks, and shards of wood scattered on the lawn. The fire in the kitchen behind them cast long flickering shadows; the sound of wood cracking in the blaze registered vaguely in the back of her mind. Nick stood staring. For a second he hesitated, too shocked to react. Then he was running, shouting back over his shoulder, "I'll go and get help, you stay here with him."

Jerry hardly knew what to do — her heart was pounding and tears stung her eyes. She placed her jacket over Ben's slight frame and tried to wipe off some of the blood spattered on his face with a tissue. She was afraid to disturb him and make things even worse.

He lay on his side, unable to move, looking up at her.

"Jerry, dear, I'm so sorry," he said softly, his voice barely audible. "This is all my fault."

"Nonsense, it must have been the stove ...," she started to say, then a thrill of horror penetrated her shock. "Oh, my god, another explosion," she whispered. She tried to control herself, to concentrate on the Professor, this was no time to get hysterical. She daubed ineffectually at the tiny cuts on his face but her mind was racing. Suddenly she grasped what he meant. He was talking about the painting. Professor Johnson had done Nick's painting — so *he* must have painted the Vermeer, too.

He tried to say something. She took his hand and gave it a gentle squeeze. "You mustn't worry about any of that now. It's all right. We know. We've just realized you did the Vermeer."

"Yes ... yes ..." His breathing became more shallow, more laboured, but he continued, "... doing it for years. This time ... went wrong ... Andrew ..."

"Don't try to speak now. You can tell me all this later," Jerry said soothingly.

"My partner ... died ... met Andrew ..." He struggled to get the words out. Jerry felt helpless, she didn't want him to waste energy trying to talk, but he seemed determined. His voice dropped to a whisper, and she leaned in closer.

"He's sick ..." He tried to swallow. Jerry found herself squeezing his hand tightly. She released her pressure; he squeezed back in response. "He tried to hurt you ..."

"Please, Professor Johnson. You must save your strength. Nick has gone for help, he'll be back soon," she said trying to affect confidence, to reassure them both.

The professor grew quiet. Jerry didn't like his colour. It was hard to see in the low light but she thought he was looking very grey. She continued holding his hand, wishing there was something more she could do. Suddenly he squeezed her hand again and looked up. "Andrew did this," he said, his voice stronger. "He knew we were together tonight ... he's obsessed ... wants to kill us all ..." Then he went limp. Jerry was looking at him with rising panic, she hardly heard the sirens of the approaching ambulance.

Someone helped her up, taking her aside so they could work on the professor. She felt Nick touch her arm as he joined her. They stood together silently, in shock, watching the men trying to revive him. Soon it was obvious there was nothing they could do. He was gone.

Chapter 25

JERRY AND NICK WATCHED IN A DAZE as Professor Johnson was taken away in the ambulance. It still hadn't sunk in. They were numbly surveying the debris in the garden while firefighters put out the blaze in the kitchen. A police officer approached them. "We need to speak with you. Can you come to the station with us now?"

Jerry lay her head back against the seat of the police car. She closed her eyes and addressed Nick who had been riding in silence beside her. "Ben said Andrew did this."

"Caused the explosion?" asked Nick.

"Yes." She quietly related what Ben had told her, and they lapsed back into silence. Jerry felt the same thick sleepiness, the same numb disbelief she experienced after her loft had exploded. Nick appeared to be in a similar state. He stumbled and seemed to have trouble focusing as they followed the officer into the building.

When Jerry described the explosion in her Toronto loft, the officer looked up sharply from his notes. "Do you think this explosion is related?" he asked.

"Definitely," she and Nick said in unison.

They poured out the whole story, trying to present it chronologically. Jerry was telling the officer what had happened in Italy, when she stopped in mid-sentence.

"Carol. Oh god, Nick. Do you think he'll be after her, too?" she cried out.

Nick sat up in his chair. "Of course. Of course, he will. Bloody hell!" he answered. "We have to phone Wiens right away!"

"Please, you've got to help us. We need to get in touch with the Toronto police immediately," she explained. "We think he'll be after my friend. Ben said Andrew would kill us all."

They had just missed him. Wiens was gone for the day. The British officer spoke to the desk sergeant in Toronto who said he'd try to reach him. Then Jerry called Carol. There was no answer at work, at home, or on her cellphone. She tried one of their friends who thought she might be at her cottage. The hysteria that Jerry had suppressed earlier washed over her in a wave. She bent over holding her stomach.

"We've got to get to Toronto. We have to beat him there. There's no time to lose," she gasped.

Nick's voice was worried. "He may be there already."

"What do you mean?" Jerry looked at him in astonishment. "He has to be here still. He only just set the explosion at your flat!"

"Jerry ...," Nick started, but the officer interrupted.

"He could have put it on a timer, love. He didn't have to be there. He could have set it hours ago."

"Can you check the airlines? Can you see if he's already flown back?" she demanded.

"Of course we can check ... But he may not have been using his own name," replied the officer, reaching for the phone. He put a call through to ask for a check of airline passenger lists to Toronto in the last twenty-four hours. While he was waiting, Jerry asked if he could get access to the passenger lists.

"If he's using a false name, perhaps I'll be able to recognize it ...," she said, not having any idea if she could, but thinking desperately that it was worth a try.

As expected, no one by Andrew's name had flown to Toronto in the last three days, let alone the last twenty-four hours.

They went to find a coffee in the reception area while they waited for the passenger lists to be sent over.

"Maybe seeing the names of all the passengers will help," Jerry said hopefully.

"He could choose anything for a pseudonym, how will we know?" asked Nick, sinking heavily onto the fake leather couch by the coffee machine.

"I don't know. I'm just ..." She looked at him, shrugging. "I'm just ... hoping," she ended lamely.

A few minutes later, the officer brought the lists to them. Jerry's heart sank as she glanced through the pile of paper with hundreds of names.

"This is impossible!" she exclaimed after they had been reading over the lists for about ten minutes. "We need some kind of system. Wait, didn't these lists arrive via the computer?"

"I think so," replied Nick, wondering what she was getting at.

Jerry was up and moving towards the officer who had given them the lists before Nick realized what she was doing. She was standing over him at his computer when Nick joined them.

"Can you export these lists to a word-processing program?" she was asking. "Nick, can you do this? I only know the software used in North America."

The officer transferred the lists and set them up at an empty desk where there was an old computer they could use. They quickly grouped all first names and initials starting with A, reasoning that he could have kept his forename. As they examined the groupings for every flight in the last twenty-four hours, Nick suddenly exclaimed in surprise, "De Mayerne! Look, Jerry! A. De Mayerne. That has to be him!"

"Why are you so sure?" she asked.

"Because De Mayerne was Ben's personal obsession. He was a seventeenth-century physician who researched painting materials. He kept a record of the materials and techniques of well-known artists while he was living in London."

"So you think that Andrew adopted De Mayerne as a pseudonym because of Ben? Like a code name between them?"

"It's the most likely name we have here. And look, he left London this afternoon, just after lunch."

"That means he does have a head start on us. He'll be there by now. What can we do?" she said, her voice thin with panic.

"We'll ask the officer to phone the police in Toronto and tell them what we suspect. They will protect Carol and look for Andrew. We have to be patient."

She tried to calm down, but she was sick with worry. "I don't think I can be patient. I don't think I can relax until I see Carol," she blurted out. "I know it's out of our hands, but I just really want to get to Toronto. I have to see her and know she's safe!" She could feel herself on the edge of hysteria.

"It's all right, Jerry. Take a deep breath and try to calm your-self," Nick said, looking grimly down at her, his hands on her shoulders. "We can go to Toronto. We can get the first flight out of Heathrow. Okay?"

They promised to keep in close touch with the Cambridge police. As they climbed into the taxi the officer had ordered for them, Nick started to tell the driver to take them to Heathrow. Jerry interrupted. "Wait, Nick. My handbag's in your flat. It has my passport — what about yours?"

Nick caught himself and gave directions to his flat. He leaned back in the seat and took her hand. "Now I'm getting as carried away as you are," he smiled. "I don't know why we're rushing. Flights to North America don't usually leave till mid-morning at the earliest. It'll be a long night. Maybe we can stay in the flat and get some sleep before we leave."

By the time they got there, the firefighters and police had gone. From the street, Nick's building looked the same. The blast had knocked out part of the back wall, but the front, which included his bedroom and study, was still intact. As they approached the front door a dark shadow detached itself from the bushes.

"Oh, Minou. Poor little cat!" said Jerry, scooping her up. "You must be very upset."

Nick swore as he entered the hall. "We can't stay here, Jerry. It reeks of smoke. Let's get our things and keep going to Heathrow."

"All right. Shall I take Minou to your neighbour?"

"Yes, please. I'll go in and start packing."

It was almost midnight. Joyce had not been to bed, she was still too unnerved by the explosion. She stood in her doorway wearing a bathrobe and eager to talk about the "accident." Jerry told her it was a gas explosion. No point in sharing the whole story, that could wait for another time. As she was handing over Minou, Nick joined them.

Joyce offered to call a local carpenter first thing in the morning to have him board up the back of the flat. Nick agreed quick-ly. Jerry could see that he had not thought of it himself, he must still be in a state of shock. We'll have to be careful. Neither of us is thinking very clearly right now, she warned herself.

They climbed into the waiting taxi. The driver had hung around, hoping for the fare. It took just under an hour and a half to reach the airport, where they discovered the next flight would not be leaving until eleven in the morning. By the time they were settled in the executive-class lounge, it was two-thirty in the morning.

They tried calling Carol again, but with no success. Jerry called the Toronto police. The same desk sergeant was on duty. "I am sorry, we haven't been able to reach Detective-Sergeant Wiens. He was due to go off on holidays starting this weekend, he may have already left," he said. "Don't worry, the case has been re-assigned to Sergeant Graham."

"What about Carol? Did you send someone over to her apartment?" asked Jerry.

"We did, and no one answered the door."

Jerry sat down beside Nick, letting out a long sigh, and told him the news.

"Of course, she's probably at the cottage," she said hopefully. "She'll be safe there. He could never find it."

"You should have asked if her car was there," said Nick.

"Damn. I didn't think of it." She got up wearily to telephone again, leaving a description of Carol's car with the desk sergeant. She rejoined Nick. "He said he'd send an officer to check out her car. I'll call back in a few hours."

"You look exhausted," he said. "Why don't we try and get some sleep. There's nothing else we can do right now."

Chapter 26

THEY ARRIVED IN TORONTO ONLY TWO HOURS AFTER they left
London — Toronto time, of course. The seven-hour flight
went smoothly and both slept. Jerry, who normally could never
sleep on an airplane, thought it was more like passing out than
sleeping naturally, but it had helped. Her mind was more at ease
since she had learned from the police that morning that Carol's
car was not in the parking garage.

They took a cab directly to Carol's apartment, and entered
through the underground garage, so she could see for herself. Sure
enough the space was empty.

"Good," said Jerry. "She rarely uses her car except to drive to
the cottage."

They took the elevator to Carol's floor. As soon as they
entered the apartment, Jerry sensed something was wrong. She
did a quick survey and saw the small desk in the hallway with its
front drawer pulled out; the contents dumped on the desk.

Puzzled, she walked over. "Carol wouldn't leave it like this,"
she was saying as she looked at the pile of papers lying in disarray.

"Nick!" she cried, her voice strangled.

She was was holding a piece of paper in her hand. All the
colour had drained from her face, her hand was shaking. "It's the
map," she said.

"What map?"

"The map to her cottage. She kept copies here. He must have
come ... he must have found one. He knows where she is!" Jerry
felt sick.

They were in Jerry's car and on the road in no time.

Jerry negotiated the traffic and sped onto the highway, heading north. They travelled in silence, each locked in their own

response to this latest development. Eventually, they started to talk.

"Why would Andrew want to kill us, especially Ben?" asked Jerry. "It doesn't make sense. He had already gotten away with the fake."

"Maybe it doesn't have to make sense," replied Nick thoughtfully.

"What do you mean?"

"Didn't you tell me that Ben said there was something 'off' about him, that he was sick, obsessed?"

"Yes. But actually, Nick, I found Andrew very together. Look at how easily he lied to me when I confronted him that time at Carol's — when he brought me the cheque. He was so smooth," she said. She manoeuvred the car into the express lane to pass a transport truck, trying to suppress the urge to put her foot straight down on the accelerator, to drive as fast as possible to get to Carol. Common sense prevailed; there was no point in killing themselves on the way to rescue her.

Nick mulled over what Jerry had said.

"*Too* smooth. That's probably it," he said, mainly to himself.

"What's it?

Nick took a deep breath. "Jerry," he started, frowning, "have you considered that Andrew could be a psychopath?"

"What, a serial killer?" she answered incredulously. "Of course not!"

He shook his head. "No, no. Not all psychopaths are serial killers. Some of them never kill at all."

"If they don't kill anybody, how can they be a psychopath?" asked Jerry, genuinely puzzled. She had only ever heard that term in connection with grizzly killings, and when Carol was trying to warn her about Nick, of course, but she wasn't about to mention that.

"I have a friend, Ron, who's a psychologist. His specialty is the study of psychopaths. We've talked about them a lot. They're quite fascinating," explained Nick. "For one thing, it appears that psychopaths are born that way — it's not a condition that develops because of their environment, or from experiences in early childhood. Psychopaths can be born into a perfectly normal family."

Jerry slowed to take the next exit off the main highway. From now on they would be on smaller roads, winding through dense forest.

"Go on, Nick."

"Well, the thing that distinguishes a psychopath from your average run-of-the-mill criminal, is that a psychopath is entirely devoid of the ability to empathize with others."

"You mean they have no feelings?"

"Not for others. They have plenty of feelings for themselves. In fact they can be quite obsessed with their own needs and comforts. But somehow they lack what it takes to relate to other people's feelings. For example, they can inflict pain without any remorse whatsoever."

"But you said not all of them kill."

"There appears to be a kind of continuum in psychopathology from mild to severe. And apparently their early environment can play a role in how they express their difference from others. If they're brought up in a family with strong strictures against acting out, and they're only mildly psychopathic, they might limit their actions to taking advantage of people."

"How do you mean?"

"Oh, embezzlement at work or stealing money from their family. Hurting people by lying to them, cheating them; the whole range of what we would call thoroughly dishonourable behaviour."

"But they won't kill?"

"Not if they're only mildly affected; then the fear of being caught, or the threat of punishment, will act as a deterrent. But if they're more than mildly affected, then the normal deterrents to killing, including moral and ethical issues just don't apply. Nothing will stop them. In fact, one of the classic signs of psychopaths is their treatment of pets."

"Please don't tell me. I can guess," Jerry shuddered.

"Yes. It can get pretty gruesome."

"So why do you think Andrew might qualify as a psychopath?"

"From what you've told me, he sounds like a very cool individual. That's a classic sign: psychopaths lie with impunity. If they're caught in a lie, they just keep changing the story. When you accused Andrew, it was easy for him to convince you he was innocent. Look at the way he manipulated you: he got Carol to let him into the apartment and had you sitting in the living room with him. Before that both of you were convinced he'd tried to kill you. Ron told me that one of the problems in dealing with psychopaths is how charming and convincing they are. They can even manipulate seasoned psychologists who are studying them."

"What does this mean for Carol? Does that mean he might play with her beforehand? What are you saying, that he could be a sadist too? Nick, I can't bear this," she said, gripping the steering wheel, her eyes on the narrow asphalt road ahead.

"Slow down, let's think, Jerry. What do we know about him already? He seems to prefer to arrange things from a distance. He chooses explosions. He doesn't get directly involved in the killing. That's a good sign."

"You mean a good sign that he won't torture her?"

"Well, yes. He probably doesn't like to get his hands dirty. And you said he's very fastidious in the way he dresses."

"Yes. He never looks creased. It's amazing." She turned off the asphalt onto a gravel road. "So he won't like the idea of blood ..."

"No, he's unlikely to shoot someone. It's probably too immediate, too messy, for him."

"Great. A cerebral psychopath," she said grimly.

Jerry had to slow down on the gravel. The car would easily go into a skid if she drove too quickly.

"I still don't understand why Andrew would come after us," she said. "He got away with the fake Vermeer. He has his money. We can't do anything. Why is he still after us?"

"That seems to be a feature of psychopaths, they're not necessarily logical. They get so caught up in their own world, they don't always think straight. He's become obsessed. Obviously he can't leave things the way they are. He must feel that we could still ruin things for him, so he has to silence us."

"So, you're saying that the fact that he has gotten away with it doesn't mean anything to him: he's bent on eliminating anything that might connect him to the fraud," replied Jerry.

"Looks like it," said Nick.

They lapsed into silence. They could hear gravel hitting the bottom of the car.

"How do you think Andrew found out where you were when he set those two thugs on you at the Nice airport?" she asked. "At least I've been assuming that he organized that. Do you think he traced you through the car rental booking?"

"Nothing so sophisticated," replied Nick dryly. "I told Ben, remember? I asked him to call his friends in the art fraud unit for me, and told him I was on the way to Nice to get rid of my car."

"So, Ben called Andrew because you were about to blow their whole set up — you knew the Vermeer had to be a fake."

"Yes, I imagine when Ben got my message he called Andrew and Andrew hired the thugs to get me out of the way for a while. To give them time to auction the painting before I could intervene."

"Then it could also have been either Ben or Andrew who organized the break-in at Oscar's lab?"

"Yes. I thought it was too much of a coincidence."

Jerry thought for a moment. "Is Oscar in danger because he found the kauri copal?"

Nick shook his head slowly. "I don't think so. Since the paint sample was stolen, Oscar doesn't have any physical proof. Surely as long as Andrew got the sample back it would be enough for him."

"What was Ben's excuse when you found out he hadn't called the police, weren't you suspicious?"

"Not at all. He claimed he never received my message. He said his answer-phone had been playing up; it seemed perfectly plausible to me. I've known Ben for years. He was the last person I would have suspected. I still find it hard to believe that he was involved in this." He shook his head and said sadly, "I can't believe he's dead, either."

Suddenly Nick sat up. "What about the police? We should've called them. This place is really isolated."

"Pass me my handbag. I still have my cellphone." Jerry reached in and retrieved it, handing the phone to Nick. "Dial 911, it's the emergency number."

Nick explained the situation to the police and had started giving directions, reading them off one of Carol's maps, when the line went dead.

"Damn!" he exclaimed. "What should we do?"

They were deep in the woods by this time. There was no hint of civilization, no opportunity to telephone unless they turned around and started back.

"Maybe they got enough from the directions you gave them to figure it out. Maybe they'll contact Wiens's office. He had a map as well, it must be in the file. We just have to keep going," replied Jerry. She felt a wave of exhaustion and frustration. She banged the steering wheel hard with one hand. "I can't believe we didn't phone them sooner! What the hell were we thinking?"

Chapter 27

THEY CONTINUED ALONG THE GRAVEL ROAD for what seemed like an eternity. Suddenly Jerry slammed on the brakes. The car slid sickeningly and came to an uneasy stop by the side of the road.

"What are you doing?" asked Nick.

She threw the gears into reverse and backed up. The car was careening on the shoulder of the road, barely under control. Again she braked sharply.

"Look!" she said, pointing to an overgrown side road in the bushes. "I think that's his car!"

They made their way over to it. Nick put his hand on the hood.

"It's still warm. He can't have been here long."

"Good," Jerry answered, "maybe she'll still be all right."

"How far are we from the cottage?"

"It's no more than a five-minute walk," answered Jerry. " I guess he didn't want her to hear the car ... that way he could sneak up on her. Should we walk from here, or try to drive closer?"

"Let's walk. Remember, as far as he's concerned, he blew us up in Cambridge. We might get some kind of advantage if we can surprise him."

They started off down the road walking quickly, feeling the sun burning into their backs. After a few minutes Jerry caught Nick's elbow and pointed silently to a small road to the left. They turned onto it; soon they could see the cottage. It looked exactly as it had when she and Carol had last been there. Deep yellow rays of sun shot through the canopy of leaves in the forest. The pale green wood on the side of the cottage was dappled with light and shade. The air was heavy with heat and the trees buzzed with the dusty sound of cicadas. It looked as idyllic as ever.

They crept closer, just making out the sound of voices. Jerry silently led the way to the back of the cottage where there was a small screened window opening into the kitchen. She and Nick crouched below it. They could hear Andrew, his voice taut.

"Carol, I'm very angry with you," he was saying evenly, like a parent reprimanding a wayward child. "You're making this very difficult for me. I only work with gas. What can I do now? You can hardly expect me to organize an explosion with this ... this electric stove!"

There was no answer. Jerry's stomach gave a lurch. Was she all right? Did he have her gagged?

Then Carol's voice. It was pitched higher than usual, but she was obviously making an effort to sound calm.

"So. You did blow up Jerry's loft. Well, well. Too bad she got away," she added sarcastically.

"Yes, pity. But she won't have survived my last operation. Or Nick, or the professor. I did things properly this time."

"You set up another explosion? Jerry and Nick ...," her voice trailed off. "Where?" she asked dully.

"In Cambridge. It was quite a challenge, but fortunately I had the right equipment." He sounded pleased with himself.

Jerry heard footsteps going into the living room. She raised her head so she could see into the kitchen. Carol was facing her, tied to a chair. Andrew walked back into the room and Jerry ducked her head quickly. She didn't think Carol had seen her.

They heard a chair being scraped across the floor, then a sigh as Andrew sat down.

"I'm going to have to think about this carefully, Carol," he said conversationally. "Some kind of an electrical fire, I imagine ... no wait. Oh, how nice! You have oil lamps. You could've knocked one over. Those things are dangerous." He sounded pleased and amused. "Now, what about the timing? If I start it now, and they calculate back ... they might realize it happened during the day. That won't do. Who burns a kerosene lamp when it isn't dark?" They heard him slap his thigh and then the creak of his chair as he stood up.

"I'll have to wait until nightfall then. In the meantime I need to get you into bed." There was a pause, then he laughed. "No, Carol, don't look so worried, and don't flatter yourself; I don't fancy you! I just need to have you in bed when the lamp gets knocked over, so you and the bed can burn up nicely."

He's raving mad! thought Jerry distractedly. She looked over at Nick. He raised his eyebrows and shrugged as if to say, "What now?"

They heard Carol's voice. "Listen, Andrew. You don't have to kill me, too. I won't tell anyone. Anyway, it's going to look awfully fishy if everyone but you ends up d ... dead," she stammered, tripping over the possibility.

"Of course it looks fishy!" spat out Andrew, irritated. "If Jerry hadn't started asking questions, none of this would have been necessary!

"Oh, screw this whole thing!" he suddenly shouted. "I'm not waiting around all bloody evening to please you! I don't care how your stupid fire got started or when! I've had it up to here with all of you messing things up for me!"

They heard him slamming cupboard doors in the kitchen. "There must be some petrol around here. Don't you have an outboard?" he demanded. "What the hell kind of cottage is this!"

Suddenly the screen door slammed and they heard his heavy footsteps crossing the wooden veranda. He headed towards the lake, muttering and swearing under his breath. Jerry and Nick remained frozen in place. Would he come around the back of the cottage, would he see them? Was there time to run in and untie Carol? What should they do?

Before they knew it, he was back, triumphant. "Look what I found!" he announced as he came into the kitchen. "Look, Carol! It's perfect!" He sounded excited, childlike. "There's enough petrol in here to fix a perfect little fire all around you. I found it over by the generator. I guess the electricity supply up here isn't very reliable, is it? Good idea to have a petrol generator," he said, as if congratulating her. "Very good idea!"

Jerry could hear the liquid sloshing onto the floor and decided she had to look in and risk being seen. Her heart was racing. What a turn of events. When he was prepared to wait until dark she had thought they would have plenty of time to think of something, to sneak up and overpower him somehow, even to go for help. Now the situation looked grim. They had to stop him.

She stole a quick look through the window. Carol, her head slumped forward onto her chest, appeared utterly defeated. Behind her, Jerry could just make out a fire extinguisher beside the kitchen door. Andrew was pouring gasoline back and forth in a line across the room, talking to himself, sounding extremely agitated.

Suddenly it came to her. It'd be a long shot, but they couldn't afford to wait any longer. She grabbed Nick's arm and whispered her plan. Then she stood up and made her way around the side of the cottage to the kitchen door. She swung it open and walked straight in. Andrew froze, transfixed at the sight of her.

"Jerry! You're alive!" he said, astounded.

"Hello, Andrew," she replied cooly. She walked over to give Carol's shoulder a squeeze and positioned herself in front of her, facing the door. Her heart was thumping, but she tried to look calm.

Andrew turned towards her, his back to the door. He grinned. Carol stared at Jerry, her mouth open in astonishment, tears running down her cheeks. Andrew reached for the box of matches sitting on the table.

"Well, this *is* a treat, Jerry," he said calmly. "Now I can kill you a third time." He smiled pleasantly, opening the box and picking out a match.

Jerry glanced down, took in the dark stains from the gasoline on his fine linen trousers, and quickly focused back on his face, hoping he hadn't noticed. He continued smiling directly at her, in his normal vague way, unaware that he might be in any danger himself.

Nick silently opened the screen door behind Andrew. He grabbed the fire extinguisher off the wall and pulled the pin just as Andrew lit the match.

"Andrew!" shouted Nick. He turned, and Nick shot a white stream of chemicals directly into his face.

Andrew screamed and clutched his eyes, dropping the lit match to the floor. Flames flashed upwards. Nick quickly aimed the extinguisher at the fire but the flames danced away from the

centre of its blast. Andrew thrashed around, howling in a combination of pain and rage. His leg barely brushed the edge of the
flames, but it was still too close, they leapt up onto his trousers.
Suddenly alight, he lunged towards Nick, pushed him aside and
stumbled towards the door. Nick, caught off balance, whirled and
fell backwards against the wall.

Meanwhile Jerry and Carol were trapped behind a wall of
flames. Nick quickly picked himself up and grabbed the extinguisher, but the chemical only stayed the fire momentarily. As
soon as he doused one set of flames, others sprang up. Doggedly
he continued, but just as he was finally making real headway, the
extinguisher began to lose pressure. As quickly as the feeble spray
managed to blot them out, fresh flames took hold.

Jerry looked on in horror. Behind her was only a small window, and Carol was still tied up in the chair. Jerry's eyes were
stinging from the smoke, her throat was closing. Carol began
coughing uncontrollably. Jerry eyed the ropes around Carol's
wrists and ankles; there was a craziness in the way they wound
around and around, too many times to count. Without thinking
anymore, she grabbed the tablecloth from the kitchen table beside
her and flung it over the fire. It partially smothered the flames. As
soon as he saw what she had done, Nick dropped the fire extinguisher, raced into the living room and grabbed a woollen
blanket off the couch. He threw it on top of the table cloth; it
worked. Flames still played at the ends of the row of gasoline
which had traversed the room, but the tablecloth and blanket had
smothered the middle where the fire had been at its peak.

Nick was over in an instant to help Jerry untie the ropes
around Carol's wrists. Jerry's fingers would not behave, she was
fumbling frantically and making little headway. Nick started in
on the ropes around Carol's ankles.

"Nick! Nick! Andrew — go after him! He'll get away!"
shouted Jerry.

"Don't worry. He was still half blind, I'm sure he couldn't get
far," he answered as he pulled out his pocket knife and began saw-
ing at the ropes around Carol's feet. "Jerry, see if you can do
somethng about the fire, the edges are still alight." She succeeded
in stamping out the last of the flames, then got a knife from one

of the kitchen drawers.

Together they worked on the ropes around Carol's wrists. After several more minutes, they had her freed. They helped her up and out of the chair. Jerry threw her arms around her and they hugged as Carol sobbed openly.

"Carol, where are the cats?" asked Jerry, gently releasing her.

"They both dashed out the door when Andrew came in. As far as I know, they're still outside."

All three turned towards the door. Andrew was out there somewhere. No one wanted to face him again.

"I'll go," said Nick. "You two stay here."

"No, I'm coming," said Jerry.

"Me, too. I'm not staying in here alone," Carol announced.

"He didn't have any weapons did he?" Jerry asked her.

"He has a knife."

"Shit," said Nick and Jerry simultaneously.

All three stood frozen, wondering what to do next. The last thing they wanted was to run into a half blind, burned version of the madman they had just encountered.

"He could be lurking around out there right now," Carol ventured. "How can we tell if it's safe to go out?"

"What about the petrol ... I mean the gasoline, is there any more outside?" asked Nick.

Jerry saw where he was going with that. "You mean he could be sloshing more around outside the cottage? This old place would go up in a second."

"No, there isn't any more. I only had the one can," said Carol.

"Anyway, surely we would hear him if he were close by. It's awfully quiet right now ..." Jerry was interrupted by a curt meow outside the kitchen door.

"Alvin! Come inside, quickly!" she ordered, opening the door. But Alvin was in no hurry. He sauntered in, briefly brushed his tail against Jerry's leg, and headed straight for Carol. He rubbed up against her legs, completely unconcerned about the tense atmosphere in the room. Tony appeared and scratched tentatively on the screen to catch their attention. He sat outside and waited patiently for someone to open the door.

"Andrew can't be around," said Jerry, letting Tony in. "There's no way these two would show up if he were nearby. Let's go out-side and have a look."

"Considering the condition he was in when he left the cottage, I'd be surprised if he got very far," Nick was saying as they stepped out onto the wooden porch.

"He didn't," answered Jerry abruptly.

"How do you ... Oh ..."

They could see something floating by the dock.

"The rocks," whispered Jerry, her voice barely audible. "His trousers were on fire. He must've run to the end of the dock and dived in. Straight into those rocks you warned me about, Carol."

Nick got there ahead of them. "He's dead," he called out.

They joined him on the dock. "Not a pretty sight," said Carol quietly, as they stood looking at Andrew's body floating face down in the clear water, a red stain surrounding his fine blond hair.

"No," Jerry shook her head. "Sad, isn't it? He was so beautiful, so perfect. But underneath ... Well, I'm sorry we all had to see what was underneath."

Epilogue

Nick flew back to Cambridge to sort out the aftermath of the explosion, leaving Jerry behind in Toronto preparing for her move to the UK. One weekend soon after he had left, Jerry and Carol were back up at the cottage, relaxing in the screened-in porch, looking out over the lake.

"He's lovely, your Nick," said Carol, as she sipped some cold white wine.

"Thanks, Carol. So you approve, do you?"

"Well, he's handsome, charming, and rich," she said, twirling the stem of her glass, "but of course, he could still have been involved in the painting fraud."

"Carol!" laughed Jerry. "How?"

"He could've been in a partnership with Andrew and Ben. Look at the timing for the break-in: you were away in Ottawa with him. How do you know he was really there on a courier-ship?"

"Oh, come on. You're just jealous, you're being ridiculous ..."

"No, listen. Andrew tried to kill you, but Nick and Ben had no idea he would do that. Nick became emotionally involved with you during that weekend in Ottawa, that's why he let you know the Vermeer was a fake while you were together in Italy. He wanted to see your reaction; when it was obvious you were not the type to go along with it, he had himself kidnapped in Nice, so you would never suspect him. And then there was Ben's painting at Nick's parents' house. You mean to tell me that Nick wouldn't have noticed the foliage the way you did?" She continued, "I think he was in on it all along."

"Carol! Stop it!" Jerry protested.

Further Reading

Knut, Nicolas. *The Restoration of Paintings*. Translated by Judith Hayward, et al. Cologne, Germany: Könemann, 1999.

Simpson, Colin. *Artful Partners: Bernard Berenson and Joseph Duveen*. Springfield, ILL: Macmillan, 1986.

Spiel, Jr., Robert E. *Art Theft and Forgery Investigation: The Complete Field Manual*. Springfield, ILL: Charles C. Thomas, 2000.

Watson, Peter. *Double Dealer: The John Blake Conspiracy*. London: Hutchinson and Company, 1983.

❧